It'll take more than ropes and whips for this cowboy to keep his bratty woman in line.

The Boot Knockers Ranch, Book 4

At twenty-three, Bree Roberts is ready to sow some wild oats. The perfect place to start? The neighboring spread — The Boot Knockers Ranch, where twenty smokin' hot cowboys deliver sexual therapy to women. The problem? The entry fee is more than she's made in a lifetime.

Only wanting to explore, she figures her tanned, toned legs will be her ticket to ride. Except Ty keeps kicking her off their land. Then she begins to suspect the reason why. He *likes* her.

If Ty spots that little vixen wrapped around one of his cowboys one more time, he's going to throw her over his knee. Trouble is, she'd like it. Catching her participating in the ranch's notorious, semi-clad corn-hole tournament is one thing, but when he finds her under their resident Dom's whip, enough is enough.

Ty won't throw a naked woman out of his bed, namely one who deserves a spanking, but showing Bree the rewards of sex mixed with a little emotion leads to trails neither of them intended to tread.

Warning: Contains a spitfire cowgirl who excels at breaking the rules, and a cowboy who lays down the law — and a firm hand on her ass cheek.

Ropin' Hearts

by

Em Petrova

Chapter One

Bree sized up the fence. As far as she could tell, it wasn't electric, so no one would find a crispy piece of Bree bacon on the forbidden boundary between the Roberts land and the Boot Knockers Ranch.

Sinking into a crouch, she extended one leg and eased it under the lowest wire strand. Then she flattened herself on the ground and shimmied over to the "dark side". A thrill hit her belly as she rolled under, at least until a sharp pain speared her scalp.

Crying out, she clapped a hand over the spot. Dammit, her hair was caught on the barbed wire. She carefully tugged the strands free while keeping an ear out for anyone who might discover her on the neighboring ranch. The guys on Daddy's ranch had been warned by her father to haul her butt back if they spied her on the Boot Knockers land.

What Daddy doesn't know won't hurt him.

Freed, she jumped up and brushed the grass off her slim, red tank top and the tiniest cutoffs she owned. When she wore them on the ranch, the cowboys gaped at her. Sure, she liked the attention, but the ranch hands weren't for her. Also, those men were *real* crusty cowboys. Not at all like the Boot Knockers who only pretended to be cowboys.

Those were fine gods of men — muscled, tanned, some tattooed. She'd stared at the brochure with their pictures so long she felt she knew every man. Some wore the lines of squinting into the sun; others had boyish faces that didn't look mature enough to do the job.

The Boot Knockers Ranch didn't deal in cattle. Sure, they dabbled in beef, and word was they had some horse stock too, but Bree knew what they really did.

They treated ladies to toe-curling sex therapy. From what she'd read in the brochure, women with hang-ups over body image or traumatic sex experiences could pay for a week on the ranch and a gorgeous Boot Knocker would take care of her.

Bree's nipples peaked under her tank top as she walked the ridgeline toward the main buildings in the distant valley below. She'd been trying since she was sixteen to get brave enough to crawl under that fence. Years later, she was determined to see the Boot Knockers Ranch for herself.

One small problem faced her—she hadn't paid to be there. She brushed her long hair off her face. It wouldn't matter that she didn't have the huge fee or that she'd never make that much money waitressing in her entire life. Her short-shorts were her entry fee.

As she descended the slope, she surveyed the land. A few people were walking between the wooden cabins with red roofs. She figured no one would look twice at a woman on their land, especially with her legs.

She was aware of the lean, curvy lines developed by years of trick riding. She'd also done the rodeo-queen gig for a couple years and had a second-place trophy. Her daddy said he was mighty proud of her, but she didn't like being second.

She got a closer look at the ranch—huge barns, a chicken coop and cabins were self-explanatory. But what were those two vast metal buildings used for?

Tingles rode up and down her spine. She'd soon find out.

She passed the largest barn and circled to the closest building. As she reached the door, her heart jerked against her ribs. She drew two deep breaths before gripping the handle and pulling it wide.

Poking her head in, she found a dining hall. Long tables ran the length of the room, with a few intimate seating groups against the wall of windows. A buffet was set up.

Hell, it looked like one of the resorts in Cancún where she'd been on spring break her second year of college.

Thank God Daddy didn't know about half the things she'd done on that trip.

The room was empty, so Bree backed out and let the door close. Sun beat down and perspiration broke out on her forehead. Damn, she didn't want to face pseudocowboy sex gods with makeup streaming down her face. She paused to pat some of the dampness away, wiping her hands on her scrap of denim shorts.

A cry erupted, echoing on the light breeze blowing through the valley. She went on high alert. Several voices joined in another cry, and she set off toward the sound.

She rounded the second building, not bothering to look inside, and drew up short. Heart racing, hands clammy, she faced the most awesome sight ever. Tanned flesh glistening in the sun, muscles bunching and releasing. Cowboy hats askew, denim riding low on more than a dozen sexy hips.

Sure, there were females among the men, but Bree didn't give them a glance as she strode right into their midst. When she passed one tall cowboy with sandy hair flopping over one eye, she slowed. His face was clean-shaven, and his gaze dipped over her legs.

"Howdy," she said, putting more sway in her step.

He gave a low whistle that raised all the hairs on her body. Her insides melted, and her hips swayed for another reason.

Damn, would he come after her? Push her against one of those shade trees and kiss her like she needed to be kissed?

A knot of men separated, giving her a clear view of the reason they were gathered here. A Cornhole tournament. As she looked on, one gorgeous specimen with back muscles rippling grabbed a sack filled with corn and tossed it. The sack bounced off the rim of the wooden target but didn't go in the hole.

A cheer went up, and the stud threw his hat down. Bree skidded to a stop.

"That ain't a piece of clothing. Take something *off*, Stowe," one guy hollered.

Bree looked between them, shocked to see the men in states of undress. Some still wore plaid shirts rolled over thick forearms. Most wore jeans, but one guy had on only boots and a pair of navy boxer shorts printed with red lips.

She focused on the front of those boxers, wishing they were tight enough to see if rumors about the Boot Knockers were true — that they were all hung like horses.

Unable to see anything, she drifted close to a man with folded arms, his biceps bulky around a carved chest. She showed off one leg in the pose she'd snagged several guys with in college. Who cared about agricultural studies when she could major in men?

Insecurity prickled in the back of her mind. God, she hoped it worked this time. For all the webs she'd cast and guys she'd snared, she'd only had a handful of sex experiences. It was like guys were incapable of following through. And those who did hadn't lived up to her fantasies. None of them turned her crank.

Which is why I'm here.

"Nice tattoo," she said to him.

He looked up, a half smile creating a dimple smack-dab in the middle of one cheek.

His eyes were warm, dark hair plastered to his forehead. Slowly he held out one arm, palm up. She eyed his palm, wondering about the relationship between hands and cocks.

The tattoo of a belt buckle had writing she had to lean closer to read. "You're a rodeo guy?"

"Six years on the backs of bulls. Made good enough scores to go professional for a spell." His drawl wasn't Texan, but, whoooeee, did it make her sizzle.

"What's your name? I bet I know you."

"Elliot James. You follow the tour?"

"Yep. Did a bit of rodeoing myself." She caught the chain around her neck, tugging until the gold pendant rose from the depths of her cleavage. Oh yeah, Elliot was watching.

He hovered over her, bringing the spicy scent of man she craved so much. He pinched the pendant between two thick fingers, and her pussy flooded with thoughts of him pushing those fingers inside her.

Breathing heavily, she tried to control her reaction. She wanted to play it cool, but it was nearly impossible. Between his muscles and those dark, snapping eyes…

His breath washed over her, and her nipples hardened almost painfully. "Trick rider, eh? Bet you've got some tricks you could show me." He pitched his voice low.

Another cheer sounded, and she looked around to see a Boot Knocker unbuckling his pants with quick, practiced movements. When his tighty-whities came into view, his bulging erection was unmistakable.

"Nice wood," one guy called to him. "Marcie thinks so too. Care to meet us in Bungalow 2 after the tournament?" The cowboy who'd drawled this had his arm around a petite brunette who blushed an alarming shade of red.

Bree felt her own face grow warm, but parts much lower grew warmer.

Elliot let the pendant fall between her breasts once more, his gaze following its descent. "Who's your Boot Knocker?"

Panic lifted in her, a wild bird in her chest. She fought to control her voice. "Oh, him." She pointed in the direction of the group, hoping it was enough to trick Elliot.

"Ty?"

"Yes, that's right."

"I'll have to have a word about getting some trick-riding lessons from his girl, then."

"Sure." The word wobbled, and a constant throb took up residence between her thighs.

"Hey, Ty!"

Bree's muscles bunched, her body preparing to bolt without a command from her brain. This guy Ty would rat her out, and they'd surely know she didn't belong here.

Think. Think. Shit.

The gorgeous man had enough swagger to knock the air from her. She watched his muscles rolling, arms swinging loose, denim pulling tight over his thighs. Six-pack, hell. Ty looked as if he had twice that.

He let his gaze travel over her body, making her quiver with excitement. He was one of the baby-faced guys, but he was hot as hell. Besides, if he sprouted a five o'clock shadow, he'd look rough and dangerous enough to suit her.

She shifted her hips, giving him the best view of her toned thigh muscle. What was she doing? She should run for it.

Daddy always said I did tempt fate. We'll see if these two men make me the filling of a Boot Knocker sandwich.

Judging by the looks on Ty's and Elliot's faces, she was in a double-good position to get her dreams fulfilled.

"S'up, Elliot?" Ty's gaze didn't leave her. In fact, it sank to her breasts then up to her face.

"Your gal here is in to trick riding, and I feel the sudden need to learn. You up for sharing her?"

Bree's heart rate spiked. Her panties flooded.

"My gal…" Ty drawled the words, and her stomach hatched a thousand butterflies.

Run for it.

No, wait it out. If I can get two for the price of one pair of short-shorts…

Ty's eyes narrowed, and his long brows punctuated his suspicion. He swaggered near and snaked an arm around her middle. When he hauled her against his rock-hard body, she felt the tension running off him.

No escape. Shoulda run.

"Not with this one, Elliot. She's all talk in bed."

She sucked in a gasp. Confusion crossed Elliot's rugged features.

Ty delivered a pinch to her backside that made her yip. "For all her shorty-shorts, she's a cold fish. But I'll meet *you* in the bunkhouse at nightfall if you want to play."

With that, Ty started dragging her away. She dug in her bootheels.

"If you don't walk away with me normal, I'll pick you up and throw you over my shoulder, *Miss Roberts*."

Ice filled her veins. He knew her. How? Was there a wanted poster on the wall somewhere? This man saw dozens of women a week—surely he wouldn't remember her face after visiting her ranch.

"Let go of me!"

"I don't think so, sugar tits. You're trespassing. Wonder what *Daddy* would think of you down here getting corrupted."

"Sugar tits! Did you really just call me that?"

He placed his mouth close to her ear, heating it with his words. "Don't you want to be objectified, sweetheart? Isn't that why you're here?"

"No." She aimed a kick at his shin, but he moved his leg at the same moment. "Where are you taking me?"

Her pulse thrummed. For the first time since rolling under that fence, fear took hold. Not because Ty would likely hand her back to her father and she'd be in for the lecture of her life, but because she might not get another chance with a Boot Knocker.

No, I'll get a chance.

This time her bootheel glanced off Ty's shin. He didn't even flinch, just kept walking.

"What do you have — iron shins?"

He eyed her. "I've got iron *everything*, sweetheart. Now I'm going to put you into my truck and take you home." With him being shirtless, she was well aware of how hard he was.

"How do you know I didn't pay to be here?"

He glared at her. Up close his eyes were green, glowing like sea glass. She shut her jaw with such force her teeth grazed her tongue. Biting off a curse, she let him drag her another ten feet before really digging in.

She tore away and set her hands on her hips. "I can go on my own."

"I'd prefer to escort you." He didn't look fazed by her anger. She felt it simmering just below her skin, about to boil over if he tried to manhandle her again.

She waved a hand as if he were an annoying fly. "Go on back to your Cornhole."

He ran a hand over his chest and abs. She stopped breathing. The sight of long fingers over ridges of manscaped flesh rendered her panties a soggy scrap.

Sure, Ty had one of those crooked cowboy smiles.

Too bad he was an insufferable jerk.

After his treatment of her, she wouldn't have sex with Ty if he were the last Boot Knocker on earth.

* * * * *

Ty had enough experience with women to know when they reacted to him. Besides, the tight peaks of Bree's nipples gave her away.

Reaching out, he nudged her jaw shut with his knuckles. "Stop drooling, sugar tits."

"Don't you dare call me that again," she grated out.

"Isn't that what you want? To use your smoking-hot body to lure us cowboys in—"

"Pfft. You're hardly cowboys." Disdain dripped from her tone. "Well, maybe Elliot

13

was a cowboy. Anyone who could sit a bull for the tour has skill."

Ty stopped walking. "We're cowboys first, Miss Roberts. Do you suppose I know your father because he frequents our beds?"

His words had the effect he desired. Her face mottled red then purple. She looked like a beet about to explode. A beet with a sweet body, not that he should be noticing. She was probably underage.

"My father would never—"

"Don't get your panties in a bunch. I was just teasing. How old are you anyway?"

She cocked a hand on her hip. Dark-blue eyes would gun down a lesser man. Not him. A veteran Boot Knocker, he could handle any female. From flighty to sad to pissing mad. One little cowgirl from the neighboring ranch didn't intimidate him.

"You think I'm not old enough to be here, is that it?"

"I *know* you aren't supposed to be here. Did you pay the fee?"

"Uh."

"That's what I thought. Now answer my question, because it's going to determine how I return you to your ranch."

14

"What does that mean?"

He lowered his jaw and gave her a hard look. "Answer me."

"Twenty-three."

"All I needed to know." With that, he sagged at the knees, locked his arms around her smooth, curvy thighs and tossed her over his shoulder. She kicked like a mule, but he was stronger.

When she pounded his back with fists that felt like a child's, a laugh escaped him.

"Damn you, Ty. Set me down!"

He slipped a hand over the curve of her tight ass, probing the fringed edges of her shorts, dangerously close to the silky flesh. She smelled sweet and soapy, the way a country girl should smell. Sometimes in his line of work, he got women trying to impress by wearing too much perfume. First thing he did was get them into the shower, and, well, they forgot about wearing perfume—or even clothes—right quick.

He continued to carry her across the grounds. When they hit the upward slope, he didn't slow.

"You're not even out of breath."

"I've carried sacks of grain heavier than you. And, *yes*, I am a real cowboy. We all are. Many of us got our starts ranchin' here in Texas."

"Not Elliot." Was it him or did she sound a little moony over Elliot?

"No, he's a country boy from Arkansas. You'd best forget about him."

She struggled, flopping on his shoulder like a big fish. Her aroused scent filled his head. A telltale heat rode low in his gut, making him instantly hard. She had one of the most luscious asses he'd ever seen, and the fact he was going to deposit her on the other side of the fence didn't sit well with his raging hormones.

He crested the ridge and walked for a long way before he caught sight of her long, blonde strands of hair dangling from the barbed wire. He swung her off his shoulder and set her down with a thump.

She popped up to her feet like an angry kitten.

"If you don't come back, I'll never say a word to your father. But if you do..." he leaned close enough to kiss her pouting mouth,

"...you'll be sorry. Now run along, Miss Roberts."

She puffed with irritation. They glared at each other for a long minute. "You can't keep me off the Boot Knockers Ranch."

"Is that a challenge?" He arched a brow.

"Take it any way you like."

When she was riled, her Texas twang was pronounced. The corner of his mouth twitched up.

"And stop smiling at me like that. Go back to the ranch and leave me alone." She did that dismissive waving motion again, and his smile fell away.

"Not until I see you go." He reached around and smacked her ass. Not hard, only enough to sting.

She jolted but didn't make a peep.

Not hard enough. She needs to be taught a lesson. Actually, he had visions of her liking a spanking too much. Little spitfire needed to be tied up. No, that train of thought was worse. His cock hardened and he resisted the need to adjust it.

He jerked his jaw toward the fence. "Get goin', sweetheart."

"It's Bree." She crouched, extended a leg and slipped under. When she bobbed up on the other side of the fence, they faced each other. "Thanks for the lift."

"Obliged, Miss Bree." If he had a hat, he'd tip it.

She snorted and rolled her eyes. Then pivoted on a bootheel and flounced off across her own field, headed toward her quaint ranch house Ty had admired when he'd visited her father. Ty watched her go, trying like hell not to notice the curves of her ass.

He had a thing for sarcastic girls, but this one was dangerous. He needed to wipe her from his mind, and quick. Then he'd go down to the tournament and miss a few more throws on purpose so he ended up naked. It was his week off, but he always had invites to bed. Elliot was a sure thing, though other Boot Knockers asked him to join them and their ladies.

* * * * *

By the time he made it back, the tournament was wrapping up. Most couples had gone off to their bungalows.

His thoughts drifted back to Bree. What was her secret trouble? As forward as she was, it was unlikely she had any secrets. Still, she might have come to the Boot Knockers Ranch seeking help.

Nah. She was just a young woman wanting a thrill. Well, she wasn't getting it from him.

But Elliot was.

The man was bent over the outdoor sink, splashing water on his face. By the time he straightened, Ty had closed the gap. He grabbed him around the middle and ground his erection into Elliot's ass. The chiseled planes ignited him, and he bit into Elliot's neck, tasting salt and man.

"It's not nightfall," Elliot groaned.

"I can't wait." He spun his fuck buddy, pinned him to the wall and kissed him.

Their mouths slammed together. With a hot rush of need, Ty drove his tongue deep, tasting, aching. He rocked his hips against his fellow Boot Knocker's.

Elliot dug his fingers into Ty's ass, hauling him closer. He burned as he flipped his tongue against Elliot's. "Got a condom?" Ty panted.

"A Boot Knocker always has condoms."

It was true. Safety came first on the ranch, with sensitivity to feelings a close second. Ty didn't need to be aware of Elliot's feelings, though. They were fuck buddies. On this ranch if somebody wandered by and saw two cowboys together, they didn't give it a passing thought.

He grappled between them, rubbing the ridge of Elliot's erection snaking to the side and down his thigh. The fresh country air filled his nostrils along with the scent of man. Ty moaned and dropped to his knees. In seconds, he had his fuck buddy's jeans open and his cock in his mouth.

Hot, salty flesh filled his throat. With strong pulls, he sucked until droplets of precome coated his tongue. When he looked up, Elliot's eyes were glassy with lust, the depths darkened by his blown pupils.

"You do that so fucking well, baby," Elliot rasped.

"Do this better." He reached around and slid a finger, unlubed, into Elliot's ass. He pushed lightly, not wanting to hurt him, but his partner liked it rough.

"Fuck yeah." Another few seconds passed before Elliot clutched Ty's shoulder and urged him to his feet. Elliot fumbled a condom out of his shirt pocket. While he opened the packet then Ty's jeans and rolled the condom onto him, Ty ripped open the pearl snaps of Elliot's shirt and lapped circles around each dark-brown nipple.

Want throbbed in him. "I need you. Now." Grasping Elliot's hips, he spun him to face the barn wall. He guided his covered dick straight at his partner's ass. He panted with the need to lose himself in that tight, clenching heat.

He flattened Elliot against the barn wall. "Feel that rough wood on your nipples while I enter you."

A full-body shiver snaked down Elliot's spine. When his chest was locked to Elliot's broad back, he entered in one slow, smooth stroke.

"Hellll."

Elliot released a hiss as Ty pushed deeper, sinking to the root. They held totally still, chests rising and falling, birds singing in the distance. Ty delivered a lick down Elliot's neck. "Okay?"

"Yesss. Now move." Elliot reached back and clamped a hand on Ty's hip.

He moved slowly at first, drawing out to the tip before plunging back in. His eyes rolled back at the amazing sensation of taking a man. From a young age, he'd known he was bi. As soon as he figured out not everyone wanted to kiss his best friend, he'd accepted he was different in that sense.

He had no inhibitions about his sexual orientation, which helped his career along. He loved his job, while racking up the bucks. A nice nest egg sat in his bank account. Someday when his hips ached with arthritis from fucking, he'd retire comfortably.

Rocking harder, his balls slapped Elliot's body. The sound was music, and he churned his hips faster.

Short gasps escaped Elliot. Ty twisted the man's face to the side to kiss him. Their tongues dueled as he pounded into him.

"I can take it. Don't hold back." Elliot grabbed Ty's wrist and placed his hand right where he wanted it—covering his thick, eight-inch cock. The length curved up and out, wetness pooled at the tip. Ty took it in hand and stroked it nice and slow as he entered him hard and fast.

"Like this?"

"Hell yeah. Is this how you fuck that little blonde?"

Suddenly, Bree's angry glare entered his head. He pushed it out and shoved deep.

Elliot grunted, legs shaking. His back muscles flexed, and what a beautiful fucking sight it was. All that warm, hard flesh. His body gripping Ty's cock.

Come spurting over his hand.

He pumped Elliot's cock through his fingers as his own orgasm rushed up. His spine tingled and the air was punched from him. A long bellow ripped into the air. Nothing unusual on this ranch.

Elliot was quiet with release, always had been, at least with him. Ty rode out the orgasm, filling the condom with hot juices of lust.

Sagging forward, Elliot quaked, the final drops of come slicking Ty's fingers.

"Mmm." Ty pressed his lips to Elliot's throat and rumbled through each aftershock. When he pulled free and turned Elliot in his arms, he brought his fingers up to have a taste of his friend.

Elliot's eyes hooded. "You're so fucking kinky."

"You love it." He lapped his fingers clean and licked his lips.

"So true."

"I still want you at nightfall. That was a quickie."

"What about that wild filly of yours?"

Ty fell still, heart suddenly tripping again. "The blonde?"

"Yeah, the one with the great legs. You said she's not very responsive, though. Maybe you just need to turn up the heat for her."

"She isn't really my client this week. I'm off."

"So am I. Weird that two of us have a week off. Usually we only rotate one at a time."

"Maybe someone backed out of their contract at the last minute. It's happened before."

"Yeah." Elliot leaned in and ran his tongue over Ty's lower lip, making his cock jerk all over again. Actually, he was still as hard as stone.

It has nothing to do with Bree and her great legs.

No, Ty was a boob man. He liked big tits he could cradle, lick, suck and later make into pillows. Bree Roberts didn't have big enough ones to suit him. So what if they were sugar-sweet, popping from the top of that red tank?

He stamped his mouth over Elliot's. "I'll see you tonight."

"You bet your ass."

With a wink, Ty took care of his condom, pulled up his jeans and walked off to find his shirt lying discarded by the abandoned Cornhole game.

Chapter Two

Bree shoved her cowgirl hat farther down over her brow, ensuring it didn't bounce off. Then she swung into the saddle and patted Royal Hoofprints's black mane. The mare tossed her head, and Bree laughed.

"Ready for a good ride?" She kicked her sides and they took off, trotting at first then galloping as the mare hit the field beyond the ranch.

Bree ran her in two loops before they got up to speed and she flipped out of the saddle. As she dangled head down, she used her ab muscles to straighten her legs and hold the pose, counting hoofbeats. The house blurred by; then it was only fence and fields.

Breathing through her nose to steady herself, she yanked herself upright again. "Good girl," she praised Royal. They'd been riding together—and doing tricks—since Bree was thirteen. The mare had listened to her yell in frustration and her speckled coat had caught many tears.

So talking to her now was the most natural thing in the world. "Can you believe that high-handed *cowboy*, Royal?" Bree spun backwards in the saddle, bouncing along for half a loop before rolling off one side and holding another pose.

"He picked me up…" she landed in the saddle once more, "…and carried me back to the fence." Damn him for seeing her blonde hairs caught in the barbed wire. She'd felt like more of an idiot.

Without thinking, she performed two more difficult tricks it had taken a year to perfect. From the distance, she heard a cheer from one of the ranch hands but ignored it. They liked to watch her and if she was honest, she practiced at this time of day to show off. What good were skills if they were hidden?

Catching her breath, she galloped for another full rotation before hooking her feet into the loops on her trick-riding saddle and standing. As Royal rolled beneath her, she focused on the horizon. She could ride for a mile this way, breeze on her face, as one with her animal.

Except she was still riled from yesterday's adventure. Being down there on the Boot Knockers Ranch had thrilled her in countless ways. After storming into her bedroom and slamming herself inside, she'd fallen on her bed and used her fingers on her pussy before pulling her small clit vibrator from her nightstand drawer and having two body-racking orgasms.

All that tanned muscle had raised a need in her unlike any she'd ever known. Too bad Ty had dragged her away. She'd had a chance with Elliot.

As she circled the field two more times, three, her mind raced ahead. After supper, Daddy relaxed in his office with the ranch foreman and a glass of bourbon. He'd never notice if she left, not that she needed supervision.

Slipping under the fence had worked fine, and she'd do that again. But she'd try to stay under Ty's radar. If he saw her, he'd tell Daddy for sure.

Her thigh muscles burned from holding her balance for so many loops and she lowered herself to the saddle.

The cowboys were driving the horses back into the paddocks for the evening. As they passed, several lifted a hand in greeting. She waved back.

Were the Boot Knockers really cowboys, as Ty had said? She'd always thought of them as being more pampered. The ranch had hot tubs, pools and silk sheets, from what she understood. The cowboys in her life slept rough in the field with hurt cows and lived on jerky during the calving season.

She shook her head. No, if the Boot Knockers had once been cowboys, they couldn't really call themselves that now. Of course, Ty's hands *had* been rough with calluses.

Goose bumps broke over her skin, and she brought Royal to a stop with the pressure of her knees. Then she dismounted and walked the horse several loops to cool down.

By the time she reached the barn, her father was there, giving instructions for tomorrow and praise for today. His men stood around him, attentive and respectful. As she entered the barn, several tipped their hats at her or grinned.

Her father gave her a sharp look as she passed. "Thought you had chores, Bree."

"I'll get to them now."

"Trick ridin' is for fun. You do your chores first."

She drew up and set a hand on her hip, looking her father right in the eyes. "I'm not ten anymore. My work gets done. What does it matter if it's within your preferred time frame?"

One of the cowpokes grunted in amusement.

Her father snapped his attention to the man with a muttered "we'll discuss this later".

Bree tossed a sweet smile at the cowpoke for distracting her father and led her mare into the stall. She stripped off the saddle and tack, then brushed the horse and gave her a treat.

As she groomed Royal, she listened to the harsher language of the men in the barn. They discussed sick animals and cracked hooves, being saddlesore and who was going into the local town for some beers on Friday night.

She thought about Ty. No cowpoke she'd ever known understood the meaning of the word "objectified", let alone used it. Ty seemed to be slightly more educated than the men she was accustomed to.

If he hadn't been an ass, she might have liked him. Her initial reaction to his chiseled body had cooled quickly when he'd called her sugar tits then deposited her at the fence and told her to go home.

Like a dog worrying a bone, her mind returned to his words. What did he mean when he'd asked if she'd come to the ranch to be objectified? Of course she didn't want that — she was a modern woman. She just wanted a chance with a Boot Knocker and if they all drooled over her, she'd have a bigger pond to fish from.

She finished in the barn and followed the men out. Dinner would be on the table, but she had chores to complete if she wanted to slip away tonight.

"See you inside, Miss Bree." One of the newer hands on the ranch gave her a crooked-toothed grin.

"Actually, I have to do the chicken coop. Tell Daddy I'll eat later."

He bobbed his head, looking as if his neck were a spring. "Want some help with the chickens?"

"No thanks." The last thing she wanted was company. She needed the time to plan her escape. The ranch hand nodded again and went inside with the others. The table would be set with Cook's hearty meal and some decadent dessert. Bree would miss out, but she had a smorgasbord of man flesh waiting for her.

After rushing through the job of gathering eggs—so late in the day some of the chickens had booted them out of the nest and she had to go searching—she stood outside the coop, checking her appearance.

Her skintight jeans and boots were a little dusty, but a pat-down took care of it. She stripped off her Western shirt and ran her hands over the cropped T-shirt. It clung to her curves, revealing a band of flesh above her jeans.

As she strode toward the fence line, she tried to imagine what the Boot Knockers were up to at this time of day. She couldn't stop thinking about Ty telling Elliot he'd meet him. Meet him for sex? Just the two of them or would they invite a woman to join them? Before yesterday, she'd never considered relations between the men.

The mere thought started a tingle between her legs. She focused on that burn, wanting so much more. Tonight she'd get it.

Slipping under the fence was a piece of cake, and much to her relief, Ty wasn't standing there like a dog guarding a coveted steak. Bree walked along the ridge and down into the valley.

Right away she came across a tall, lean cowboy. He had his shirt off, tucked into his back pocket, and his hat askew as he emerged from the barn. A second later, a woman—older than him, by the looks of it—walked out buttoning her blouse.

Bree's libido revved. She wanted a romp in a barn. Hell, she'd take a romp in the chicken coop if it meant having fun with a sexy man who knew what he was doing. Judging by the satisfied smirk on the woman's face, her tall-drink-of-water cowboy was skilled.

A shiver gripped Bree as she wandered between buildings. She still didn't know what was inside one big metal building, but no one seemed to be in the vicinity, so she took another path.

As she spotted a smaller building, she stopped in her tracks and pressed herself against the nearest wall. A huge cowboy was gathered outside with a muscled man wearing a black shirt and black hat standing close.

"Coming home for supper?" the man in black asked.

The other cowboy gave a nod. "Tell Sybill I'll be there but don't hold food for me. I need to check on something."

"What's that?"

"I heard someone tampered with a certain cowboy's toy cupboard again and he blackened another guy's eye for it."

"Damn, really?" The man in black laughed.

"Not funny, Archer. I'm going to have to give him a week off for fightin', at this rate. He's split Jeremy's lip, shoved Blake into the horse stall and now this."

"Yeah, you're right." Riggs Archer kicked at a tuft of grass. "Need to get the guys to work on this lawn. The heat's killing it."

"Not much we can do about the weather in Texas." The bigger man turned and started striding away, his muscles a delicious sight Bree couldn't tear her gaze from.

"Hugh."

The man turned to Archer. Something passed between them, hot and primal. Bree's nipples puckered and she sucked in a breath.

"Don't be too late." The insinuation in his tone sent a wave of lust crashing over her.

"Get Sybill ready for me," Hugh rumbled then continued on.

Archer watched him go for a long heartbeat, before circling the building. A minute later Bree heard an engine start. An ATV shot across the field, heading up the ridge toward the big house.

Breathing hard, she tried to make sense of the connections on this ranch. Those cowboys were obviously together. And they shared a woman? When Bree had first planned to snag a Boot Knocker, she'd only hoped for one. Now she was burning to score two.

* * * * *

"You heading to supper, Ty?"

He looked up at one of the new Boot Knockers. In less than a year they'd lost five from their ranks, and this cowboy had been one of the first new hires. The rookie fit right in with them — Ty just didn't know him very well. Only that the ladies claimed he was amazing at oral.

Ty dug his pitchfork into the hay and pitched it into the horse trough. "Yeah, soon." He knuckled away a rivulet of sweat escaping his hat, darkening his work glove. "You go on. Tell Cook to keep a couple of baked potatoes for me."

He loved baked-potato night. He'd load two with cheese, bacon and chives then douse them in sour cream. That was one of the bonuses of the ranch. The meals were gourmet every day. Sure beat the crap he'd grown up with. His momma had been a terrible cook. He, his two brothers and their father had grumbled through every meal until the week Momma went on strike.

After seven days of cereal and burned toast, they'd learned to swallow her cooking without complaint.

"See you at the grub house." The man threw him a wave and left Ty alone in the barn.

He'd begun his chores late today. Worn out, he'd been slower than normal. He'd barely fed the horses before he'd had to break up a fight between two guys. More practical jokes gone awry. Most of the time, the pranks were funny. Hell, he'd eventually laughed about his own eyebrow being melted off with cream while he'd been asleep. But some people weren't good sports.

When Hugh heard about the scuffle, he wouldn't be happy. Ty shook his head and forked more hay.

The action soothed him. Maybe it was lack of sleep, but he'd been edgy all day. As if his shirt was too tight across his shoulders or he had a piece of hay in his undershorts. Something was rubbing him wrong.

He knew what it was but didn't want to acknowledge it.

Miss Bree Roberts.

Sassy, sexy and totally unwelcome on this ranch. She wasn't paying, and she couldn't be here. He should have marched her back home to Dan Roberts and let her daddy deal with her.

She was young, though, and Ty recognized the desire to sow wild oats. Hell, he still was. Women came here to do that very thing, but Bree needed to stay on the other side of the fence.

Sweating freely, he set the pitchfork back in its rightful place and checked the horses one more time. Following a meal of loaded baked potatoes, he'd grab a rod and head down to the pond. Dip a line and maybe catch a bass or two.

As he left the barn, he pulled off his gloves and shoved them in his back pocket. His wallet was already there, bulging with condoms after restocking following a night with his fuck buddy.

That was another thing bothering him. He'd overheard two guys linking his name with Elliot's the way they did Hugh and Archer. It wasn't at all like that. He loved his job, and he'd never jeopardize it with a strong bond like Hugh and Riggs had.

In the past year several Boot Knockers had lost their heads for female clients or each other. Hugh and Riggs had dropped from the ranks first, followed by Damian. He was married and had a new baby, happily running his own photography business. And recently Jack had finally convinced Paul to give them a chance — and roped a pretty filly, Lissy, into the deal.

They couldn't afford to lose Elliot, and it appeared that man was searching for someone to attach himself to. Ty needed to back off and make sure Elliot knew what they had was casual sex. No strings.

Evening was descending earlier now, the sky streaked with pink and purple. The week was wrapping up, and soon there would be fresh blood on the ranch. In a few days he'd have his own woman to peel off the ceiling after amazing bouts of sex. Right now, he was going to enjoy an evening of downtime. Baked potatoes, fishing…and an early bedtime for once.

The grub house was hopping. Guys lined the benches, their ladies curled up beside them. When Ty entered, Elliot waved and pointed to the bench. Ty raised his jaw in acknowledgment, but he wasn't in the mood to hang out with his friends.

His thoughts strayed to Bree once more. He bet she'd be into a threesome with him and Elliot. If he did invite Bree to his bed, his friend was the only one he'd trust to keep the secret.

No. He couldn't allow his mind to take that path. She was too young, her sassy mouth too irritating. She had no business here on the ranch, let alone in his thoughts.

Or his bed.

How many times was he going to repeat these things to himself? He'd have to keep her away from Elliot too. The man had been far too interested in her.

Once Ty had a plate heaped with potatoes and a bottle of beer, he wandered back outside. He'd find a spot on the grass and enjoy the cooler air and quiet.

The ranch spilled out before him, a postcard image. Hills, valley, pond. Someday he wanted a piece of land like this to call his own.

He stuffed himself with chives and bacon goodness to near explosion then downed his beer in one continuous swallow. After returning his tray to the grub house, he went back out to the storage shed to find a fishing rod.

The walk to the pond was peaceful. The body of water was the center of the ranch. Lots of guys brought their ladies down here. They held picnics and bonfires as well.

As he ducked through some trees, he spied a couple taking advantage of the solitude. Two slim figures cut through the water. One splashed her partner.

Feeling like a voyeur, Ty sat down, facing away, behind the trees and waited for them to crawl up the bank. Their laughter sounded along with a playful slap and a yowl of surprise.

Several minutes later, the couple walked back to the ranch, arms around each other. With the coast clear, Ty came out of his hiding spot and threaded his hook with a rubber worm.

Five casts later he felt the tension ease from his shoulders and his breathing deepened. Lately the ranch had begun to feel a little small. Twenty Boot Knockers and just as many women and a handful of personnel. Not to mention the threesomes now inhabiting the ranch and a few hired hands. A man couldn't get a few minutes of solitude.

He drew his brows together, staring at the spot his line entered the water. He adored his job and living on the ranch. What was his problem today?

Probably lack of sleep. Yeah…

A giggle made him jerk the line. Looking around, he caught sight of the tree branches moving. Another feminine laugh. Then a rumble from a man.

Damn. Didn't even catch a fish and I gotta sneak away.

A boot flew out of the trees and landed ten feet away from Ty.

He glared at that dark-brown leather cowgirl boot. Instant fury leaped in his chest.

Damn it all, Bree's back on the ranch. After carrying her over his shoulder, he'd recognize those boots anywhere.

Tossing aside his rod, he stormed up the bank. Grabbed the boot. When he broke through the trees, he set eyes on a round ass in hot-pink panties with bows on the sides. And a Boot Knocker was busy untying them.

"Hey!" Ty hurled the boot. It bounced off the cowboy's shoulder and the lovers twisted to see who was throwing things at them.

Bree's face went through a transformation—eyes widening with terror, cheeks flooding with color. Finally her features settled into a look of blazing anger.

But Ty was angrier.

He started toward them. Bree locked a hand over her breasts, which had been bared, her bra straps hanging loose off her shoulders.

"No point in covering up those sugar tits, sweetheart. I've already seen them. And so has he."

"What the hell's wrong with you, Ty?" The Boot Knocker, Cameron, was one of the youngest among them. Because he was still thinking with his dick, Ty wouldn't tell Hugh he was screwing around with Bree.

"Get outta here if you know what's good for you." He stared at the cowboy's surly expression. When the man didn't move, Ty gritted his molars together. "I said, get out." His voice was low, hot with barely harnessed rage.

"She's your girl? Hell, she was all alone. I didn't know."

"Yeah, and she's gonna stay all alone." He reached for Bree. She brought a knee up to root him in the berries, but he leaned away. "Get your clothes on."

Her long, blonde hair seemed to float around her head as if controlled by her emotions. She jerked her bra back into place. As she reached back to hook it, Ty's balls clenched tight. For a second he drowned in images of burying his nose between those B cups and inhaling her. And later clutching the mounds together to create a sheath around his cock.

Ty looked away, at the Boot Knocker's retreating back. He was carrying the clothes he wasn't wearing.

"How far'd you get with him?"

"Not far." Her twang grew more pronounced.

God help him, her panties were slipping down her thigh, the front fluttering open. He clamped his hands into fists to keep from grabbing those skimpy pink ties and knotting them. If he had his way, he'd construct a rope chastity belt for her before sending her back to her daddy.

"You're like some kind of ranch guard dog," she snapped.

He stared at her profile—rounded cheeks, button nose. Sultry lips. In another few minutes those plush pink lips would have been all over Cameron.

Ty huffed out a breath. "When the ranch needs guarding from young country girls who don't belong here, yeah."

She threw him a glare before yanking her top over her head. Blonde hair caught in the neck, but she didn't bother to pull it free. Instead, she tied up her panties then poured herself into the tightest jeans he'd ever seen.

"What are you gonna do with me?" she asked, pulling up her zipper. He felt every damn vibration of the metal teeth in his groin. Hell, this woman was going to kill him.

"You're going home."

She met his gaze, gray-blue eyes flashing. A heartbeat passed between them, long enough for him to get control of his arousal and remember his irritation.

"Get your boots on."

"Do you do anything but boss people around? 'Get out of here, get your boots on.' Do this, do that."

"I take charge when it's necessary. Otherwise, I can be the best friend you've ever had."

Her blue gaze slid his way as she tugged on a boot. "I doubt that." The minute she had both boots over her trim calves, she took off.

He caught up to her in a few strides, feeling the effects of seeing her ass in tight jeans and remembering the silk fluttering away from her pussy, revealing a shadow of hair.

Taking her by the upper arm, he forced her to walk beside him.

"I'll leave on my own."

"I don't trust you. See, you've tried to steal from us twice now."

She whirled, hair flying. A strand caught on her lip, drawing his gaze. "Steal?"

"Yeah, what we have to offer is a service you must pay for. You're trying to take without paying."

"What are you, the business manager?"

"No, but this ranch is my life. I'll do whatever I can to keep it profitable."

She snorted and tried to pull her arm free. "Do you have a damn business degree now?"

"Yeah, I do."

Her step faltered.

"You think we're all dumb muscles down here, don't you? Not really cowboys. And we don't have brains." His shirt really did feel too tight now. He felt he'd burst the seams as his lungs puffed with anger. It didn't help that each breath filled his head with her sweet, soapy smell.

When she didn't respond, he went on. "I've known girls like you before."

"Yeah? What am I like?"

"Entitled. You think because your daddy has money you deserve whatever you want. Even if you have to take it."

"Not true," she bit off.

"Why don't you ask your father for money for a Boot Knocker of your own? Or would Mommy be disappointed in her precious daughter paying for a man?"

She stopped dead, and he almost yanked her arm. When he looked at her face, he saw what he'd said was very wrong. Tears sparked in her eyes. "My mother is dead. Cancer, my third year of college."

"Shit, I'm sorry, Bree."

"Shut up, you ass."

He released her arm and they walked across the field toward the ridge. He felt like a real piece of shit. Why did she rile him so much? He normally kept his cool, but she got under his skin.

"I lost my grandmother to—"

She cut him off. "I don't care. Leave me alone, Ty."

He liked her mad at him rather than hurt *and* mad. "Whatever you say, sugar tits."

That did it.

With a roar, she turned and launched herself at him. He watched her fists battering his chest, for a blink before gripping her wrists and pinning them behind her back. She twisted in his hold, resorting to using her sharp, little cowgirl boots.

He looked deep into her eyes. "If you kick me, you're gonna be sorry."

"If you call me sugar tits again, *you* will."

The corner of his mouth quirked up, which pissed her off more. For thirty seconds, she fought like crazy. He held her, spitting out blonde hairs and taking the occasional knee to the thigh.

It was the most exhilarating moment he'd had in a long time.

"All right, all right. I won't call you that anymore. They *are* sugary good, though."

She sagged in his hold. "They're small."

Startled, he stared at her. Bree was bold and overconfident to the extreme—at least on the surface. It appeared Miss Great Legs might not be so in love with herself, after all. She had hang-ups about size. Most likely, because the media supported women with huge breasts and disproportionate waists, she'd fallen into thinking she was inadequate.

"Size doesn't make them less tantalizing, sweetheart."

With a grunt, she tore free. She ran up the ridge and he caught her at the top. In silence, he walked at her side as they made their way to the place where she'd shimmied under the fence.

"I got it from here," she said without looking at him.

"Make sure I don't see you back on this ranch. Next time I *will* tell Daddy."

She shot him a glare then dropped down and performed a perfect roll beneath the barbed wire. When she gained her feet, she took off in a run, silhouetted by the sun, running back to the place she belonged.

"Bree!"

She turned.

"I promise never to call you that again."

She must have known what he was talking about. With a wave, she started running again.

Smiling, Ty crouched and skimmed a finger over the blonde hairs still caught in the wire.

Chapter Three

Elliot crowded onto the bench beside Ty. The warm, familiar length of thigh against Ty's made him look up. Elliot's gaze met his.

From down the bench, the words "Ty and Elliot" reached him.

Shit.

Ty inched away a bit and spooned his morning oatmeal faster.

"Where's your lady this morning?" Elliot asked. If he felt the wall Ty was trying to erect, his tone didn't reflect it.

"Wore her out," Ty said around a mouthful. He eyed his friend, and they shared a grin.

"You got that sweet little brunette, didn't you? Jill?"

"Yep." He grabbed his orange juice and drank half of it.

"What's Jill's reason for being here again? I remember reading something different on her cut sheet before we started the week."

"She has unusually long orgasms," Ty said.

The Boot Knockers across from them perked up their ears.

"Like how long?" Stowe leaned over his plate of eggs.

Ty could leave them hanging, but finding a woman who could orgasm for nearly an hour straight was like discovering an oil geyser.

"Her last orgasm was thirty-eight minutes."

"What the…" Stowe whistled low.

"Are you shitting us, Ty?"

"Nope."

"And she's here why? Obviously she has little trouble getting off."

"Because the men she's been with have called her a liar, saying no one can be in a euphoric state for so long and she must be faking." Usually Ty specialized in women with skewed body images, and having this little lady was refreshing.

"Damn, that's harsh," Elliot added.

"It's made her wary of sex, but after last night, I think she's cured," Ty said.

"Can she orgasm more than once a session?" Elliot asked.

"Oh yeahhh," he drawled.

"What do you do while she's coming? Kick back and watch TV?" Stowe looked a little more tired than normal, and brackets were formed around his mouth. For the past few weeks, he'd seemed a bit depressed. Ty hadn't seen Stowe even joke around. He wondered if it was a particular client who'd tied Stowe in knots — instead of the other way around.

"Hell no. I keep things going."

"How?" Elliot asked.

"Hold her, caress her. And getting a blowjob by a woman who is still coming from the barest touch of your fingers is pretty damn hot."

The guys whooped.

"Damn," Elliot said. "Wish I'd gotten Jill. Deana only wants to talk."

All eyes turned to him. Talking was fine — as long as it didn't go on endlessly. Judging by Elliot's expression, this was the case.

"Talk about what?" Ty asked.

Elliot issued a sigh. "Mostly she talks about her ex and what an asshole he is."

"How long has she been out of the relationship?"

"Four years."

"Ugh, definitely needs a firm hand," Stowe said.

The man would use a crop, paddle and whip on a woman like that. He still didn't sound very enthusiastic, though.

"You think?" Elliot cocked his head.

Ty jumped in. "Yes. She's waiting for you to shut her up."

"Negotiate a scene where you can tie her up and spank her ass. See if that doesn't stop her from thinking of her ex."

Stowe's advice was sound. Ty had a little experience with women like Deana, and typically they were searching for someone to take control and shake them out of their destructive behavior. The Boot Knockers saw plenty of women clinging to anger or memories of a dead relationship.

Elliot set down his fork, looking ready to jump to his feet. "Do you really think that's all she needs? I'm sick and tired of talking. She's beautiful and soft, and, well, I haven't been laid for four days."

"Better get back to work then, Elliot," Ty said.

"Yeah, I will. Thanks for the advice, guys."

When he left, several others at the long table went too, leaving Ty alone with Stowe. Looking at his friend, he noted dark circles beneath each eye. That was the norm when they were all sleep deprived, but something else was wrong.

"Want to talk about it?" Ty asked.

Stowe barely roused, shaking his head once. "Won't help."

"What's wrong, man?"

Stowe scrubbed his hands over his face. When he raised his gaze, he looked bleaker than ever.

"If you've got client problems, I'm pretty good at making suggestions."

"That's not it. She's fine."

"Not as responsive as some?"

"No, she isn't." His voice was gritty. Abruptly, he climbed off the bench and grabbed his plate. "See you later, Ty."

As he walked away, Ty watched his leather-clad ass. As their resident Dom, he wore leather well. Too bad he rarely played with men. He got off on being in command of females.

Ty finished his OJ and bussed his dishes. Then he went out into the sunshine. He'd left Jill fast asleep. After keeping her twitching most of the night, she must be exhausted. He'd let her rest and rejuvenate.

Some construction was taking place on the ranch—cement pads being poured for a few more bungalows. Hugh had just hired five more guys. Either he was covering his ass in case they lost more lovesick cowboys or they were turning a lot of women away.

It was good business sense to expand, and Ty agreed with the decision, not that Hugh had asked. Maybe when Ty was done having fun as a Boot Knocker, he could get into the business end of the ranch. He stood and talked with the cement crew for a few minutes then headed up to the ridge.

For a week he'd been walking the fence line, looking for signs of Bree. The grasses weren't tamped down and no more blonde hairs hung from the barbed wire. Did that mean she'd been a good girl and stayed on her own property?

He looked in the direction of her ranch. With her rebellious attitude, he doubted she was behaving. Dan Roberts didn't have very much control over his daughter, but maybe that was due to her losing her mother.

When he thought about the pain in her eyes at his mention of her mother, he still felt like an ass. Yet she'd shaken it quickly and given him her sharp tongue.

Hell, why was he still thinking about her?

He'd been trying to figure out why she'd burrowed into his psyche. The only thing he could decide on was how much he wanted to teach her a lesson.

His thoughts spiraled out of control, complete with visions of her panties trapping her round little thighs together and her tight ass in the air as he reddened it for her.

The Boot Knockers all had kinks and spanking had never been one of his, but thinking of Bree's ass under his hand made him as hard as steel. Maybe he'd return to Bungalow 14 and wake up Jill.

Throwing one last look in the direction of the Roberts ranch, he shook off lingering visions of the spitfire. They were both better off if she didn't trespass.

* * * * *

Mother of mud-splattered man chests, Bree had picked the right time to sneak onto the Boot Knockers Ranch. She had to give her brain the order to close her mouth—the view was *so* pretty.

Tanned gods on ATVs, slicked with mud as they raced through a patch of field far away from the buildings. And they were all in their underwear.

Some women were stripped to bras and panties, arms wrapped around their cowboys as they ripped up the earth. Tonight Bree would put a notch on her cowgirl belt.

I'm gonna get me a piece of that.

She removed her boots and jeans, glad she'd worn her red panties. With any luck, they'd stick out to the Boot Knockers like a flag before bulls. She dropped her top to the stack of clothing and ran barefoot onto the field. Mud oozed between her toes and her feet made suction noises with each step.

But her panties were already growing damp. The Boot Knocker she'd almost made it all the way with last time spotted her. *Let's finish what we started,* his expression said.

She jogged forward just as he made a loop of the field and came straight at her. He slowed, hooking an arm around her waist. She jumped onto the back of the four-wheeler and wrapped herself around his hard, lean body.

He tossed her a devilish smile over his shoulder. "Howdy, Bree."

She tightened her hold around his middle, her internal engine revving at the feel of warm muscle. "I'm ready to ride."

"I bet you are." He gunned it. The ATV shot right into the fray. Bree was splattered with cold, wet mud. Against her burning skin, it almost felt erotic. She ran her fingers down his washboard abs — speed bumps that would barely slow her down once she got ahold of him. She wasn't leaving the ranch until she'd gotten what she wanted.

As the man whipped the four-wheeler around, mud splashed over her leg and foot. Another Boot Knocker wearing mud-drenched underwear and a Stetson pulled up beside them. The girl on the back grinned at Bree, squealing when they shot off.

Bree's driver gave the ATV gas and they raced after, weaving back and forth through the mud, drawing dangerous crisscrosses. Bree whooped with joy as they reached the other four-wheeler.

Just as they neared, her Boot Knocker cut hard to the side, spraying the other riders with mud. The other woman laughed, mud clinging to her hair and dripping down her face. Damn, where else did an adult get to play like this? No wonder these women paid so much for a week on the ranch.

She scooted closer to the hard male in front of her, pressing her pussy right against his ass. He pushed backward and she skated her hand down his abs to the thing she wanted most.

His cock was rigid. She followed the hard flesh from the base to the mushroomed tip, outlining it through his mud-dampened boxer briefs. He groaned and clamped a hand on her thigh. As he inched his fingers toward her soaking center, he drove faster. Hopefully headed off the field to a more private place.

From her peripheral vision, she glimpsed a blur of movement. Then her Boot Knocker was gone, wiped off the vehicle. She cried out, trying to process what had happened and take control of the ATV. Scooting forward, she gripped the handlebars, braking hard.

Bodies rolled, and a driverless ATV rolled to a stop near hers.

It only took a heartbeat to understand. Ty and the man she'd been playing with were locked in a wrestling hold. She jumped off the four-wheeler, sinking into the mud to midcalf. Pulling each leg free took a lot of energy, but she made it over to the writhing male bodies.

"Son of a bitch!"

"Dickhead."

"I'll punch out your goddamn teeth." Ty's growled oath raised all the hairs on Bree's body. He cocked a fist, but the other man rolled at the last minute. Ty's fist sank into the blackish earth.

Grunting, Bree's Boot Knocker flipped, pinning Ty beneath him in a hold more erotic than anything she'd seen. His groin was locked to Ty's ass, and Bree's thoughts stampeded. At least until Ty reached under the other man's arm and ripped it out from under him.

They rolled, came up sputtering then went down again.

"Stop!" She jumped up and down. "Leave him alone, Ty!"

They continued trying to beat the hell out of each other, the blare of ATV engines going all around them, oblivious or uncaring that two guys were trying to drown each other in mud.

Bree stuck her fingers into her mouth and issued a shrill whistle. Ty looked up, eyes greener than ever within his muddy face. His expression was fierce, an avenging angel's. Shivers began deep inside her, but these weren't vibrations of arousal.

He was going to take her to Daddy.

She twisted on her heel and ran for it.

She hadn't gone five steps before a big body slammed her. She fell, flat out, spread-eagle, with two hundred pounds of angry cowboy crushing her.

"Umph."

"Get off her," Bree's cowboy ordered.

She tried to move, but Ty was too big, too heavy.

And so damn aroused. God, he felt huge. The small ache in her pussy swelled to epic proportions. Without thought to how much she hated him, she arched upward.

"Damn you, Bree." He bit her earlobe—hard—leaving her dizzy and out of sorts until she realized he was on his feet, and he and the man who was interested in her were trying to pound each other into the mud again.

Ty swung, catching the other in the jaw. Cameron's head rocked, but he stood his ground.

"Damn idiot." She pushed hard to unsuction herself from the ground. Thick mud pasted her entire front, and she spat some out, disgusted by the grittiness in her teeth.

Her cowboy came at Ty, eyes blazing. Her hero hooked the annoying man in the gut, but Ty didn't even wince. Instead he stared at Bree, a vein throbbing beneath the mud coating his neck.

Shit. The instinct to run burned, but he'd only catch her again. She eyed the closest abandoned ATV, escape in mind. She'd gun it to the top of the ridge and roll under the fence.

As she pulled her foot free, Ty's voice boomed over the ruckus. "Don't. You. Dare."

With a display of primal strength, he grabbed the man and tossed him aside as if he were a pillow. Then he came at her.

She backed up, mired in the dirt, shaken. No, *shaking.* She stared at Ty's furious face and wondered what he'd do to her once he got her.

She couldn't let that happen. With a shot of raw adrenaline to her system, she took off. Behind her, his feet slurped in the mud, seeming slower than hers. But he caught her way faster than she'd thought possible.

A rock-hard arm locked around her middle, yanking her off her feet. She shrieked as he carried her across the field, her legs churning in the air.

"If you're gonna act like a child, I'll treat you like one." His voice was guttural.

He set her down and she'd barely figured out she was on solid earth when freezing water hit her skin.

She gasped then screamed. Icy spray seemed to carve into her skin. Mud ran down her body and shivers took hold. She tried to block herself from the harsh hose water, but Ty was determined.

When the water hit her breasts, pleasure warred with pain. She crossed her arms, and he lowered the jet stream to her belly. She loosed a scream that she hoped brought every cowboy on the ranch running, but no one came. She tried again, and Ty directed the water at her face, filling her mouth.

Spitting, she tipped forward, letting water run out. He gripped her upper arm and spun her, giving the same treatment to her back. He painted stripes of water over her skin, taking a long time on her ass, which probably was pretty damn caked with mud. But still.

"Asshole!"

The water pounded her flesh, around the curve of her ass and right between her legs. Need sliced through her.

Before she could react to the wave of lust, he shut off the water. Grabbing her arms, he turned her to face him.

She backed up a step.

"You'd better not try to get away from me, Bree. Because you don't want to feel my wrath."

Danger alarms sounded in her head even as her want mounted. Was he going to harm her? No one had ever laid a hand on her, but he looked capable of it. His eyes were fever-bright against his muddy face.

"Stand there while I hose myself off. If you move a single toe, I'm going to make you wish you'd obeyed."

A quiver took root in her stomach, and she could only stare as he stripped off his clothes and hosed himself, fist clamped on the nozzle as he gave himself the same rough cleanup she'd received.

Her skin felt flayed. She was freezing and spitting mad.

And more alive than she'd ever felt.

Water struck Ty's broad chest, licking over tanned pecs, brown nipples, down to his more-than-six-pack abs. He avoided hosing the carved length of his cock but cleaned up his legs.

"Want me to get your back?" she shot out, only half-angry now.

"You aren't supposed to move, remember?" His dark tone speared her, and her pussy seemed to swell.

When he squirted between his toes, she found her voice. "Who the hell do you think you are?"

He shut off the water and with tense movements looped the hose neatly. "I'm not a man you can walk all over."

She snorted, and his gaze flashed to hers, pinioning her like a bug. She sucked in a gasp, heart racing.

"Now," he said tightly, a muscle in the crease of his jaw flickering, "I'm going to take you to the bunkhouse and get us both some clothes. Then I'm taking you straight to your daddy."

Hell, she was in for it. She whirled, but he caught her arm, fingers biting into her skin oh-so perfectly. Her pussy squeezed, fantasies playing in her head of her wrists being locked under his hands as he drove his thick cock into her.

Her breaths came faster.

"My clothes are over there."

"I don't give a damn. You're not getting within fifty steps of that field. If you do, you'll end up on the back of another ATV and I'll have to pound the shit out of that guy too."

A shiver sluiced down her spine.

He drew near, hovering, smelling like man and desire. "Now you will walk with me to the bunkhouse as if we were walking into a mall together."

"If I don't?" Her words ended in a squeak as his stare crashed over her.

His chest plastered against hers as he brought his lips to her ear. "You won't be able to sit down for a week."

She walked. But she couldn't stop thinking about his threat to spank her.

When he dragged her into the bunkhouse with him, she stopped short. The space was empty and smelled surprisingly fresh compared to the bunkhouse on the Roberts ranch. Maybe because the men rarely slept here.

Ty towed her down the center aisle to a bunk with a gray-and-blue-striped quilt. A small wooden nightstand stood beside it, bearing a photo of a ranch house with figures in front of it, too small to make out.

"Me and my brothers when we were young," he said as he dug into a bottom drawer. He tossed clothes onto the bunk— jeans, T-shirt and plaid button-down. He thrust the latter at her. "Put that on."

She did, grateful for the cotton's warmth after being turned into an ice pop under the hose. Her fingers were too cold to button the shirt easily. Ty watched her for a moment, still naked and wet and steaming mad.

"Let me do it," he growled, clasping the buttons. She let her hands drop, watching his face as he buttoned her into his shirt. It hung midthigh, the sleeves dripping over her fingers.

He met her gaze. Panic and heat crawled through her belly.

He stepped away and she watched him jerk worn jeans over his chiseled body. He let the fly hang open while yanking on his shirt.

Her gaze dipped to his crotch.

"I can't fit it into my jeans yet, in case you're wondering."

"You're probably too turned on by that cowboy holding you down with his cock against your ass."

He didn't even blink. "I do love a man in my ass, but that's not why I'm hard right now."

Dark need gripped her, making her almost pant. She stared into his eyes for three eternal heartbeats.

"You like the thought of me with a man, don't you?"

"I don't care what you do or with whom."

He made a noise in his chest. "You wish you could watch me sinking deep into a man's tight ass." Each drawled word licked her senses.

"I'm leaving."

He palmed his cock, stopping her in her tracks. "You ever see a man jack off?"

She wanted to look away, but he held her enraptured. She couldn't drop her gaze if she tried. He curled his fingers over the length still bulging from the V of his fly. Wetness pooled between her legs.

"You wanna see a man stroke his cock, pulling the come up from the base so it gathers on the tip?"

God yes.

He drew nearer, crowding her against the foot of the bed. One push and she'd be on her back. What then? He was angry and it would be angry sex.

That sounded exciting. Pressure built inside her.

"Is that what you want, Bree? Or maybe you want me to throw you down and sink into *your* ass?" He reached around her and clamped a hand on her cheek. She bit off a gasp. He kneaded, hard, too hard. But a good hard. She felt the fight begin to leave her.

He stepped away.

"You aren't gonna experience any of that, because you're going home."

She felt as if ice water had splashed her all over again. She pursed her lips and narrowed her eyes. "You can't keep me there."

"Your father can."

She laughed. "He wishes."

Ty didn't respond, only grabbed her arm and hauled her behind him, all the way out of the bunkhouse and halfway across the grounds to a shed.

* * * * *

Damn little vixen was going to get her spanking yet. She refused to hold on to his middle as they sped up the hill on the four-wheeler, which was fine by him. He didn't need her to like him — he had dozens of women every year who did.

Her behavior was terrible and her disregard for rules worse. She needed her mouth washed out with soap and then she should be made to listen.

Probably the only way to shut her up was to have two fingers buried in her and his tongue on her clit.

His balls were tight to his body, and his cock grew another fraction. Bree's warm thighs were close enough to touch, but damn if he'd be doing the touching.

That jackass rookie wasn't either, if Ty had anything to say about it. Ty's fists had talked pretty loudly, and he hoped the new Boot Knocker got the message this time. When he'd spotted Bree flying across the field on the back of Cameron's ATV and the man's hand creeping toward her pussy, Ty had seen red.

He'd probably get a week off for fighting, but he didn't give a damn. It was worth it.

When they reached the spot Bree normally sneaked under the fence, he zoomed right by.

"Where are we going?"

"To your house."

"Daddy won't be there. He's at auction today."

"I'm willing to wait."

"Don't you have some lady to fuck or something?"

"God, you have a filthy mouth." *Maybe she needsd it plugged with something to shut her up.*

Where were these thoughts coming from? He'd never felt so driven to take control of a woman before. Maybe because she infuriated him. Or he wanted to make her contrite at last.

Some strange need welled in him, unlike anything he'd felt before. It fascinated even as it repelled him. He was a straight shooter— helped ladies, gave pleasure. He'd delivered a few playful spanks in his career, but nothing like he was thinking with Bree.

He cut to the left hard, forcing her arms around his waist. She held herself tensely, but he knew she was gagging for him to touch her.

Let her burn.

That thought amped up his need.

As he rode along the ridge, he tried to shake the desire mounting in him. As soon as she opened her mouth, the flames were dampened.

"I bet you do a terrible job as a Boot Knocker. I'd never choose you."

Do not rise to her. Do not— "Why the hell not?"

"You don't have any focus. I'm assuming you have a woman in one of those bungalows, and you're too busy with me."

"She's plenty satisfied, sugar t—" He cut off, remembering his promise not to call her that.

She released her hold on him, scooting back on the seat so they were touching as little as possible. Fine with him.

"I've never seen you with a woman," she continued. "You either neglect them or you're not even a Boot Knocker. You're just a ranch hand, pitchin' hay all day long."

He reached back and grasped her wrist. Pulling her hand around his front, he placed it directly over his aching cock. "I do plenty of work. You only wish you could be on the receiving end."

She yanked her hand free, though her breathing grew heavier. "Arrogant asshole."

"Call me that again and see what kind of punishment I dole out."

"Assssshoooole."

He stopped the ATV. For a long, shaking moment he drowned in images of throwing her over his lap and yanking up his shirt she wore to lay hands on that hot ass. Warming the cheeks, making them red. Maybe she'd beg or shed some tears.

"You like to push buttons, but I can't be pushed."

"Every man can be pushed with the right exertion." Her words tickled his ear as she leaned close.

Manipulation wouldn't work on him. "I'm the only man you'll ever meet who can stand strong against you, Miss Roberts."

"That so?" She trailed her tongue over his earlobe. His cock jolted and his nerves were live wires, but he didn't move a muscle.

He made sure his voice was strong. "Your charms won't work on me." With that, he hit the gas again. The ATV rolled along the ridge to a gate where he could drive onto the Roberts ranch.

Behind him, Bree was silent and still. When he pulled up in front of the long ranch house, she jumped off and started walking fast. He caught her before she slammed the front door in his face. With her arm in his grip, he said, "Point me toward your daddy's office."

"He won't be—"

"Then we'll sit and wait for him." His tone brooked no arguments.

They reached a heavy walnut door. "Open it," Ty commanded.

With a small sigh, she did.

Good girl.

For a second he bowed over her, inches from burying his nose in her straight, blonde hair and inhaling her fragrance. He straightened and led her inside.

"What's this?" Dan Roberts looked up from his books, glasses perched on his nose.

"This is me returning your daughter with a warning for her to stay off the Boot Knockers Ranch."

Chapter Four

Bree had stood quietly while Ty told Daddy everything she'd done. She'd withstood Ty's glares and ignored her father's. He'd be angry for a while, but soon she'd be in his good graces again. She was all he had left.

But she couldn't get Ty final look out of her head.

Green eyes dark with warning. Why did he make her feel clammy and needy when he was ordering her around? Even the icy water digging into her flesh had done something strange to her. Her knees had almost felt weak.

She stripped off his shirt and laid it aside on her bed. Standing in damp bra and panties, wearing goose bumps, she stared at his shirt.

She picked it up and brought it to her nose. The fresh scent of laundry soap filled her head, but under that she detected Ty's male musk.

Annoyed, she threw the shirt on the floor and padded to her bathroom. According to her father, she'd be spending a lot of time on the ranch, but she wasn't twelve and couldn't be grounded. If she wanted to leave, she would. Maybe it was time to get her own place. She was flirty enough to get good tips waitressing or bartending—enough to get a decent apartment.

She took a hot shower while replaying the events of the day. Giving up on the Boot Knockers Ranch wasn't an option. Sooner or later she'd find a way past Ty and get what she wanted.

As water and body wash trickled over her heated flesh, she wondered what she really did want. If she just wanted sex, she could go down to the bar, pick up a cowboy and get off.

But that strange pressure she'd known back in the bunkhouse with Ty and all the way home hinted that a simple fuck wasn't what she wanted.

She'd only skimmed the surface of activities on that ranch. They weren't only having mud races or games of Cornhole. Darker things took place down there, and she was determined to experience them.

Her nipples were sharp peaks, her pussy throbbing. She teased her nipples until her pulse spiked, then plunged her fingers into her pussy. The slick folds parted, her walls clenched. She ground the heel of her hand into her button as she thrust her fingers in and out.

She knew just how to get herself off fast, but her cravings wouldn't be satisfied this time. Ty's growled commands were too fresh in her mind, his power so absolute that he'd made her stop and take notice.

While she drove her fingers faster, she didn't think of the cowboy she'd almost slid in to home base with at the pond. He seemed boyish compared to Ty. *I'm the only man you'll ever meet who can stand strong against you.*

Swirling her fingers faster, she focused on that deep inner point his words had touched. She rose rapidly, climbing up the steep slope toward a release so big she didn't know if she could muffle the cry.

God, you have a filthy mouth. He'd almost sounded as if he liked it.

She came fast, hot juices spilling over her fingers. She worked them hard, spreading her pussy and grinding her pulsating clit into her body. Sagging against the tile wall, she heard the echoes of Ty's words as her body hummed for more.

Chapter Five

Ty needed to pound into something. Lust rolled through his veins, gaining in momentum as every second ticked by. When he'd left Bree in her father's office, she'd given him a look that almost tore away his last thread of control. Big blue eyes, pink lips parted — a plea.

Damn her.

Ty strode past the bungalows, his mind on finding release from this need Bree had saddled him with. A bungalow door opened and Elliot's hard body appeared. He stepped onto the small stoop, seeming to take up the entire square.

"Ty."

"Where's Deana?"

"She's asleep." Pride slithered over Elliot's face.

"Good," Ty grated out. "I need you for something."

Elliot nodded and jumped to the ground. Ty strode away, knowing his friend would follow. When they reached the barn, Ty rounded on him. Grabbed him by the shirt and muscled him against a stall.

Pushing his throbbing cock against Elliot's groin, he kissed him. Elliot moaned and opened to him. Ty thrust his tongue inside, swirling around the hot depths. The dial on his need switched on to High.

As he gathered the flavors, he couldn't stop the words from tumbling from his mouth. "I want to taste her on you."

Elliot grunted. "Who?"

"Bree. Make you lick her until she screams to finish her off, then tease the hell out of her by kissing you, taking you right in front of her."

"Hell." Elliot wrapped an arm around Ty and pushed against him.

Ty grabbed his face and looked into his eyes. "I want you fucking her while I fuck your ass. I want—" he tore off Elliot's hat and shirt, "—you both to know who's making you come."

Elliot fumbled with Ty's clothes, and in seconds they stood with jeans around their boots, cocks in hand. Ty thrust his hips forward, bringing their lengths together. He wrapped a fist around both.

"Ffffuck." Elliot's eyes rolled back and his mouth fell open. Ty took advantage, kissing him with long, sucking pulls as he mimicked the action with his hand. Their bodies slapped together as they ground into each other inside Ty's clenched fist.

"Baby, let's find some hay. I want to suck your cock." Ty pushed Elliot back, walking in small steps since their legs were trapped. When he found a spot, he planted a hand on Elliot's chest, fingers splayed over one nipple.

Elliot rumbled in a way that ignited him. He pushed him down on the hay bale and followed, swallowing his cock right to the root. Elliot's hardness striking the back of his throat made him ache more. He imagined Bree on her knees, taking him as Ty leaned over his partner and sucked him.

Dammit, he had to get her out of his system. If using her right now in his fantasy while pleasuring Elliot exorcised Bree, he'd be happy. He lapped Elliot's shaft, riding under the soft spot to pull noises from his friend.

Elliot gripped Ty's nape and drew him down again and again. "I thought of you while I fucked Deana."

Ty glanced at the rapture on Elliot's handsome face.

"Thinking about sharing her. Sharing all women. I think about you all the time, Ty."

Shit, he didn't want that. At the same time, it sent a thrill through him. Someone wanted him for more than a week.

He released Elliot's cock and licked down his balls. He sucked them both into his mouth gently, rubbing his stubbled jaw over the tender space beneath his sac. Elliot cried out, straining upward, cords standing out on his neck.

"You want my cock buried in your ass, don't you?" Ty rasped.

"Fuck yeah."

He flipped him, found a condom handily in the jeans still around his ankles. Then with one long, slow thrust, filled Elliot. For a moment, Ty battled the urge to come. He gritted his teeth and took several breaths through his nose.

Elliot's back muscles flexed and for some reason Bree's wide-eyed, pleading expression popped into Ty's head.

He jerked forward. Elliot groaned, and then they were moving together. Perspiration broke out on Ty's chest, suctioning him to Elliot. Heat climbed from Ty's balls upward, tingling, burning. He closed his eyes and drew in Elliot's scent, but somehow Bree's soapy smell clogged Ty's mind.

With a cry, he came. Long, violent spurts that yanked harsh noises from him. Elliot's ass clenched around his length, his whole body shaking. Ty had the presence of mind to reach around him and take hold of Elliot's streaming cock, even as he thought of Bree's ass gripping him.

As they caught their breaths, Ty rested his nose against Elliot's shoulder. His partner shuddered. When Elliot turned his face to look at Ty, something passed that was undeniable — at least on Elliot's part.

The man liked Ty more than as a friend and fuck buddy. He'd said he thought of him often.

Ty pulled free, emotions warring. As he removed the condom and dressed, Elliot tossed him glances.

"Why don't you ask her to join us for real, Ty?"

He didn't pretend not to understand. "She lives on the neighboring ranch."

Elliot pulled his shirt back in place. "Have you had her?"

"She doesn't belong here."

"No, but she's grabbed hold of you, hasn't she?"

Shit, was it that obvious? Hopefully only to Elliot because they were such good friends.

"She's not coming back to the ranch. That was a fantasy I was talking about. You know I don't get attached."

Elliot set his hat back on his head, eyes dark, lips swollen. The side of his neck was red from Ty's beard burn. "I know that. If you want to make that fantasy a reality, I'm your man."

He nodded, throat tight as burning need swept through him all over again.

Elliot smoothed a broad thumb over Ty's eyebrow, which had finally grown back after a Boot Knocker had used depilatory cream on it while Ty was asleep. "You look better with both eyebrows. See ya later." Elliot swaggered past Ty with a smile.

Ty dug his thumb and forefinger into his eyes, trying to make sense of what was happening to him. When had he lost his precious grip on control?

* * * * *

From the set of his shoulders, Bree knew who was standing at the fence. She tapped her heels into Royal's sides and the horse shot forward. As she closed the distance between her and Ty, Bree's heart knocked.

He looked up at her approach, squinting against the sun. Drinking in his rugged features, low-slung jeans and Boot Knockers logo T-shirt stretching perfectly across his broad chest, her breathing hitched.

His hat sat askew, and she folded her fingers more tightly around the pommel, itching to set it right.

Or tear it off.

"Lookie who showed up. You planning to slip under the fence, Miss Roberts?" His drawl did things to her. Like wet her panties and turn her nipples into twin pebbles.

She glided off horseback and her boots hit the grass. "I wouldn't leave my horse here while I sneaked in."

He eyed her, amusement branding his hard lips.

"What are you doing up here?"

"What's it look like? Fixing the fence so you can't sneak in again."

"How'd it get broken?"

"Good question. Mighty suspicious that the post is tilted right here. Oh look—there are also blonde hairs stuck on the barbed wire."

"Pfft. I never touch the fence when I come under. Not since that first time."

He shoved against the wooden upright and the sagging wire pulled taut again. "My guess is you tried to jump the fence with your horse."

At that, she laughed. Not a chuckle—a long belly laugh that made him stop and stare. Hell, he probably thought she was nuts. What did she care?

After she'd controlled herself, she said, "You think I can't jump a measly fence this high without knocking it over?"

"Don't rightly know." He stared at her another beat then wiped perspiration off his upper lip. The sun glinted off the moisture, highlighting the darker stubble there.

"You can't really keep me out by mending the fence, you know."

He didn't look up, only gave her a view of the top of his hat and wide shoulders. Each push and pull tugged his shirt in ways that melted her insides.

When he finally raised his head, his face was serious. "What is your deal? Aren't you busy doing better things than chasing cowboys?"

It stung to reply. "It doesn't take long to feed chickens."

"I'm sure your daddy has you doing other things."

She shrugged. "Don't think he trusts me."

His voice dipped low, inviting new need in her. "That's not it. You're smart. He's spoiling you and he doesn't realize that's the last thing you need." He took a step in her direction as if a fence weren't separating them. His big chest came up against the wires.

"And you know what I need because — what? — you've known me all of four hours?"

"I figured out what you needed in four minutes, sweetheart."

His words were dark, stormy, and sounded a hell of a lot like an oath. Instead of backing away, she inched closer and wrapped her hands around the wire between barbs.

Ty leaned in, inches away, close enough to kiss. "You don't look like you believe me."

She laughed again, but this time she didn't feel the humor. "No one gets me, let alone some sex therapist who hasn't even had sex with me."

"I don't need to have sex with you to understand you. I bet I can write a dissertation about you after spending ten minutes in your company."

She stepped away from the fence, giving him room. "Prove it. Come across and we'll take a walk."

He shot her a grin—a slow, easy flash of teeth—that made her feel she was sinking into the earth, boneless and helpless against those pearly whites. Abandoning his tools he'd brought up to mend the fence, he bent and slipped between two upper wires. His shirt caught but before Bree could help, he was free, standing before her.

"Mighty nice on this side of the fence," he said.

She giggled. "Let me grab the reins. I don't want Royal wandering back home and making people worry I'm lying somewhere hurt." When she walked away, she put extra swing in her hips, hoping he was looking.

Royal whickered as Bree took the reins and tugged her into a slow walk. Ty strolled beside her.

"A good horse," he said.

"The finest. Royal's my girl, aren't you?" She patted her animal's neck, getting a head toss in response.

"And a little vain, I see."

"What's wrong with vain?" Bree countered.

"Nothing, except eventually her coat won't be so shiny and her legs will grow wobbly."

Bree snorted. "I know exactly what you're saying."

"What's that?" He drifted close enough that her shoulder brushed his arm. Her skin seemed to lift to his heat.

"You're saying I'm too focused on my looks and when they fade, I'll be left with nothing but my character."

"See? You *are* smart."

"My character is fine. Strong as steel."

"I have no doubts, Bree. It's you who doesn't believe."

She stopped walking and gaped at him. "I believe. If I didn't believe in myself, who would?"

"Your father, for one. And you don't want to be alone forever. You'll want a husband and a family."

She rolled her eyes. "Not for a long time. I'm not ready for settling down."

"Me neither."

"I bet having a new woman every week is every man's dream."

"For many, yeah. But it's not about the sex in those cases either. For some women, it's learning to love themselves. Proving they're pretty inside, even if they feel the outsides don't meet the world's rules of beauty."

"What do you do for those women?" They crossed the field, angling toward the opposite corner. It would take them a long time to walk back, and she was okay with that. Talking to him felt nice.

"There are many ways to show women they're worthy."

"But most of those ways involve several screaming orgasms a night."

He threw his head back and laughed. Her breath trickled out in a wheeze as she watched his whole body react to her joke. Thick neck exposed to the sun, shoulders relaxed, arms easy at his sides. He was a beautiful man.

He found her staring. "You better wipe that idea out of your mind, Bree."

"Oh you're a mind reader now? How do you know what I'm thinking?" Her voice rang with irritation. Why did he annoy her so much? He was like a boy in junior high who didn't know how to ask her out. Instead, he just teased her and annoyed her until she kicked him in the shin and walked away.

Maybe that's why he did it. He was trying to shake her off.

"I don't need to read your mind. Just your face."

What did she look like? She tried to blank her expression.

He grunted a laugh, lips tilted higher on one side. "Your pupils are dilated and you just wet your lower lip."

As if summoned, her tongue darted over her bottom lip again. Ty faced her, eyes burning. Very slowly he smoothed his thumb over her lip, tugging the skin with the calloused pad. Heat bombarded her body, slicking her pussy and yanking an invisible string connected to her nipples.

She needed to put distance between them. Needed—

"I know a wanting woman when I see her, Bree." He held her captive with his gaze and touch for another heartbeat before pivoting and walking again.

She fell into step beside him. Royal shied a little, obviously picking up on Bree's agitation. Her horse knew her better than any creature on earth.

Though Ty seemed to be doing a pretty good job. Damn him.

"I can't believe you don't have some smart-ass response to what I just said."

What could she say? She *was* wanting. Needy, hungry, aching. But Ty wasn't going to be the cowboy to ease her. In fact—

She grabbed the pommel and swung into her saddle. Royal tensed in excitement, ready to ride.

Ty tipped his head back to gaze at her. "What are you doin'?"

"Going home. And it's time you did too, Boot Knocker. You're trespassing. Get off my land." Her tone was light enough that he only laughed. Arrogant jerk. She'd half hoped he'd take offense, as she did whenever he kicked her off his ranch.

"You really asking me to go?"

"Not asking—telling. Goodbye, Ty." With that, she spun her horse and shot off, angling away from the house. She needed distance and time. The last thing she wanted was for Daddy to question her agitation or the blush she was certainly wearing.

She ran far and flat out. Praying Ty was getting a long look at her as she threw him out of her thoughts for good.

* * * * *

The minute Ty walked into the auditorium, he was met by the rhythmic slap of the whip. Stowe stood on the darkened stage. Alone. Something was definitely bothering the man.

Ty sauntered up the center aisle and came to lean against the stage wall. Stowe's whip never paused, though he looked up and acknowledged Ty with a nod. So many women loved the BDSM life. They melted under Stowe's power and control. While Ty knew little about the intricate workings of the lifestyle, it fascinated him.

The cat-o'-nine-tails slid across the stage right in front of Ty. "Ready to be my slave?" Stowe joked.

With a laugh, Ty hooked a boot onto the stage and climbed up. "Have you ever had a male sub?"

"A time or two, but it's a soft woman I need. Seeing her cry and beg for me to give her what she needs..." Stowe trailed off, staring across the stage.

"You want to talk about her?" Ty asked.

He started and swung his gaze around. "Who?"

"Whoever's got you so unfocused."

Stowe's expression rippled with something Ty couldn't name. "Did you see how I hit the center of that bench every time with my whip? You call that unfocused?" As if to prove his point, he snapped the leather again. It flicked out and struck the padded bench where a woman's ass would be.

"I see." Ty didn't press the issue. The Aussie would talk it out if and when he was ready.

"What are you here for?" Stowe was always direct and sometimes came across as brusque. But Ty didn't mind. He watched his friend store his whip in a big black chest and padlock it shut.

Ty tried to put his thoughts in order. But, as always with Bree, they were scattered. She really *was* driving him crazy if even he couldn't put words to what he wanted to say. He prided himself on being in touch with his emotions, which was why he was good at his job. Because he knew himself so well, he identified the problems his female clients suffered from and was able to present their troubles to them in a way that helped them better understand themselves.

Stowe arched a brow at him. "That bad?"

"No. Just that confusing."

"Ah. Male or female?"

"Female," he said at once. Bree's face popped into his mind's eye as he'd seen her last, giving him that *look*. Narrowed eyes, twisted lips. It made him want to punish it right off her pretty face then fuck her silly.

"I'm here to find out what's wrong with me." His words seemed to echo in the empty space. Stowe eyed him before gesturing to the bench. Ty took a seat, ignoring the thought of all the women who'd been pleasured while bent over the soft leather. Stowe hooked a boot around the leg of a short stool and dragged it close. He sat and waited for Ty to speak.

"There's a woman. I don't know what to do with her exactly."

"If you're coming to me, you must have an instinct about what she really needs."

Yep. Straight and direct.

"She's…" What was Bree? A pain in the ass, cute beyond belief even when she was writing checks with a mouth that she wasn't willing to pay for with her butt. Or maybe she was. Ty shook his head. "She needs her ass spanked."

Stowe didn't laugh at the revelation. He took spanking and punishment seriously, which was exactly why Ty had come to him, even if the decision hadn't been conscious.

"Have you doled out this punishment?" Stowe asked.

"No."

"But you want to. The power makes your head spin a little."

Damn, his friend did know his stuff. That was exactly how Ty felt. He nodded slowly. "She drives me to it. Her mouth… God, she's smart-mouthed. She won't shut up, even when she must see she's digging herself deeper. And she won't listen to me and stay where she belongs."

"That's because she's enjoying the hell out of running you around in circles."

"No shit."

"No, really. Listen to me." Stowe rested his elbows on his knees and leaned forward. Ty was reminded of having serious talks with his own brothers but, being oldest, he'd never been on the receiving end. He sat up and listened.

Stowe continued, "In her own way she's making you react because it's what she needs."

More confused than ever, Ty shook his head. "I don't understand."

"She mouths off and you react, saying you're going to make her do something, maybe even saying you'll spank her. Is that right?"

"Yes."

"But you've never followed through with your punishment, have you?"

"No. She's not mine to punish."

He pushed back and stared at Ty. "Maybe that's what she's asking of you, man."

Something forbidden sprouted in Ty's chest. Before he'd blinked twice, the kernel had grown into a full-fledged vine, tangling him up.

"She's young, right?"

"Yes," Ty answered.

"But she's all woman and knows how to use it."

"You've seen girls like her before?"

Stowe nodded. "She wants to be taken seriously as a woman and maybe nobody gives her that. It's a need she wants fulfilled. She also wants rules and she's acting out because she wants you to set them."

"Me?" Fuck. He tore off his hat and spun it counterclockwise, the way his thoughts always swirled when thinking of Bree. She made him feel out of sorts—and so fucking good. The idea of setting boundaries for her and making her adhere to them gave him a woody.

"Girls like her want to act like just that—girls. But they want to be viewed as strong women. They don't know how to meld the two, and there's no rule book that states they *should*. We come in all shapes and sizes. She just needs both sides admired and acknowledged, as well as loved."

"What...what would you call this?" Ty asked.

"I'd say," Stowe said slowly, "she needs the care of a Daddy."

Ty stared at him, trying to process what he was saying. "She has a father."

"No. I mean a Dom. Daddy and Dom are interchangeable here."

Ty pressed his lips into a hard line, feeling as if he were on a roller coaster and about to hurl.

"She sasses you, is that right?"

"Fuck yes," he ground out.

"She's encouraging you to play with her. The play she wants is punishment, boundaries."

"Why?"

Stowe lifted a shoulder. "Some women just have the need inside them. Others have suffered from some lack in their lives or a trauma that brings it out."

Ty's thoughts shot to Bree's mother, lost too soon. He swallowed against the protective lump that rose in his throat. After a few beats, he said, "I don't want to be anyone's daddy."

"This isn't about age-play. She wants care and guidance, intimacy and someone to nurture her while she acts like a sexpot. On the same note, deep down she wants to please someone. You."

Ty closed his eyes, breathing hard. How sick and twisted was it that he *wanted* her to *want* to please him? Of all his years working with women, he'd never encountered anyone as complex as Bree.

He opened his eyes to find an amused expression on Stowe's face.

"It's a power exchange. She has power, does something naughty. You punish her and then you hold the power."

"It's what she wants?" It was a half question, half epiphany.

"Give her what she needs — unconditional love, reliability, nourishment of the soul — and see if you aren't both rewarded." Stowe stood. "But, Ty? Your brat needs a firm hand." He shot Ty a wink and strode offstage, leaving him alone in the shadows with thoughts of Bree and a hard-on like stone.

* * * * *

Ty was going to throttle her when he found her on the ranch again. But she didn't care. She straightened her shoulders and walked into the grub house.

Cowboys looked up and one tipped his hat at her. Another gave her a wink. Damn, the Boot Knockers were a flirty crew. But she found herself scanning the room for one face.

When her gaze settled on it, her stomach did a backflip. Ty was sitting with a few guys, talking and laughing. As she watched, he stuck a thick hamburger in his mouth and chomped off a bite no man should be capable of chewing. But he did. Even the way his jaw worked was sexy. And when he swallowed, his tanned throat working, she pressed her knees together.

As if feeling her attention on him, he looked up. His expression blanked and he stood. When he started toward her, she backed up a step. Heart racing, panties wet.

"You'd better try to get away before I teach you a lesson." The heat in his voice infused her with want. He grabbed her by the elbow and directed her out into the cooler evening air. Without a word he marched her across the turf. His silence unraveled her and she opened her mouth to say something smart. But for the first time in her life, she couldn't think of anything.

He led her past the barns and through a small stand of trees. The wind whistled through the branches, whispering warnings to her that she was unwilling to heed. She was exactly where she wanted to be and no one — especially Ty — was going to scare her away from getting what she wanted.

When they broke through the trees surrounding the pond, she dug in her heels. "Why are you taking me here?" Visions of him picking her up and tossing her in fully clothed jumped into her mind. After the harsh hosing off he'd given her, she had no doubt he was capable of leaving her dripping wet in the pond.

He slid his fingers down her forearm to her hand. Entangling their fingers, he said, "Sit and talk with me, Bree."

If she weren't already standing still, she might have pulled up short. Talk? About what? Damn, she was in deep trouble now.

Was it her or were his eyes warmer than usual? He tugged her hand and she followed like a puppy after its master. He sank to a dry spot on the bank and patted the space beside him. Angling a worried look at him, she did his bidding.

"What do you want to talk about? I didn't know Boot Knockers had thoughts that don't deal with being naked. Are you sure you're even capable of having an entire conversation in English?"

She waited for the sparks in his eyes or his annoyed retort. Neither came.

"Would you like me to switch to French?" He spit out a string of words that melted her core. "Or Italian?" This time when he spoke the foreign words, her nipples hardened.

She peeked at his profile, seeing him cast in a new light. She shivered at the new complexity beneath the gorgeous man beside her. "How do you know all these languages?"

"Rosetta Stone."

She studied his face for signs he may be joking. "Really?"

He laughed and his face transformed, creases forming at the corners of his eyes in a way that seemed to etch into her being. "No, not really. I had an Italian grandmother and she taught me early how to cuss. I studied the rest of the language in college. As for the

French..." he dropped a lazy wink, "...I learned that for the ladies."

She wrapped her arms around her knees and tipped her head up to the vast sky.

"Do you know any languages?"

"No. Nobody really took me seriously in school. I was the dumb blonde—the cheerleader. I didn't care about making good grades as much as I cared about my social life."

"You earned your degree, though. You must have buckled down in college."

"Yeah, but Daddy never changed his view of me."

"It's hard to break out of a mold once people see us in a certain light." The tone of his voice suggested he didn't see her in that same light. What did he see in her?

They sat for a while, not speaking. Finally he lay back and his hat tumbled off. She skimmed a finger over the brim, burning with something she didn't know how to voice.

He yanked a lock of her hair and she squealed. Laughing, he pulled her down to lie next to him. He felt good, strong and solid. And he smelled divine.

"See that cloud? It looks like a turtle." He pointed and she followed his long arm to his tanned finger. She nodded, her cheek brushing the warm, soft cotton of his shirt. He kept talking. "My younger brother got a turtle once on vacation at the beach. Brought it home in a cardboard box and put it in his room."

"What was its name?"

His eyes crinkled more, and she devoured each delicious line with her gaze. "Picasso."

"What kind of name is that for a turtle?"

"My brother loved *Teenage Mutant Ninja Turtles*. They were all named after artists, so he found another artist to name his turtle after. He was always in to art, even as a little kid. He's at Texas A&M right now, finishing a degree in art history."

"He must be smart to get in there."

"It's my alma mater." He gave her another crinkle-eyed look that seared her panties.

"What about your other brother? There were three of you in the photo in the bunkhouse."

"Tommy just graduated from high school and has his sights set on becoming a Boot Knocker."

She shifted closer, lured by his voice and the comfort of just lying here talking. "Would that be weird, having him on the ranch too?"

"Nah. We'd have to be careful to stay away from each other, though. Absolutely no sharing."

She longed for him to flip onto his side, lean over and kiss her. But how to urge him to do that? She stared at the clouds, unable to see any shapes within the cottony puffs.

"What happened to Picasso?"

"Well..." his drawl slammed her with desire, "...the turtle came up missing one day."

"Oh no."

"We found him, don't worry. It was in an unexpected place, though."

"Where was that?" She couldn't resist pushing onto an elbow and leaning over him. Staring into his face was much better than cloud gazing.

"The turtle ate lettuce and my brother got distracted while feeding him. He left the bag in the turtle's tank. When he remembered to put the bag back, he didn't look closely. He tried to put the bag into the fridge and Mom said to leave it on the counter—she needed a little lettuce for sandwiches."

When he released a low laugh, Bree's nerve endings sat up and took notice—but her heart did a slow somersault she felt to the tips of her toes.

"Mom reached into the bag and found Picasso."

Bree giggled.

"My brother got grounded for a week. If he'd put Picasso in the fridge…"

She gave a shiver of mock horror.

"My brother tried to fight off the sentence, pleading his case. It only dug him in deeper. Mom was a tough one to argue with."

Bree rested onto her back again, her mind deep in her own childhood arguments. Especially one. It still niggled at her.

"The last fight I had with my mom was over the phone."

He grew still. This time his silence was a gift. When had someone truly listened to her?

"I was at college. Some friends were going to San Diego for a weekend and I wanted to go." She swallowed down the burning guilt at how she'd spoken to her mother that day.

"Your parents weren't in agreement?"

"No, they weren't. I yelled at my mom and said…she wasn't taking care of me anymore.

The least she could do was put money in my account for a long weekend getaway."

Ty was hovering over her suddenly, eyes soft. Her chest did an emotional stutter thing, coming against his, but he didn't move or tell her not to be upset that she'd fought with her mom.

"That was our last conversation before Daddy called and told me about the cancer." Her voice sounded small and wispy. But Ty heard.

With extreme tenderness he directed a lock of her hair behind her ear then leaned in and kissed the spot between her brows. She let her eyes fall shut, drinking in the man he truly was. He wasn't judging her or making her feel more guilt than she was already burdened with.

She slipped her hand around his nape and held him close, just breathing the same air. After five breaths, unease stole over her. She didn't like sharing that time in her life, not even with her father. And she really didn't like remembering.

She couldn't let this be her last statement to Ty. Her brain caught up and she found she did have a smart remark to bait him with.

"Did you forget to take your pill today?"

"What?" He pushed away to stare into her eyes.

"Your blue pill. The one that keeps you going. You have a willing woman alone and you're not even aroused." She pushed upward against his hips, noting a leap against her lower belly that said she'd spoken too soon.

"I don't need a pill to keep me hard." Amusement quirked his lips upward.

"No?" she taunted. Damn, he was like cowboy crack and she was suddenly a junkie.

"Nope. I can go all...night...long."

His drawled words and the intense way he looked at her dialed up her need. But instead of taking her, he pulled her to her feet and took her back to the fence.

"I'd tell you to stay off the ranch, but I know you won't, Bree. So I'll just say 'see you later'." He dropped her a wink she would feel the repercussions of for days.

* * * * *

The country singer's powerhouse note trilled through the bar. Couples revolved on the dance floor and cowboys were bellied up to the bar. Bree leaned back in her chair, bored out of her mind.

She pinched the straw in her fruity drink, between her fingers, and stirred. She had as much interest in her beverage as she did this scene. In her college days she'd gone to bars like this looking for some fun, but now...she felt far removed.

The kind of fun she was looking for was on the Boot Knockers Ranch.

In the past month since her escapade in the mud with Ty and — what was his name? — she'd come to realize she needed something more than what she'd been originally searching for. The other Boot Knocker was a hunk but she needed more than a fun romp.

Like something Ty had given her with only his words and looks. Hell, even that hosing off had revved her engine. Why?

She'd been trying to figure that out, with no luck. And she'd had plenty of time to think. She'd attempted to keep her father happy by hanging around the ranch and acting like the perfect daughter. Tonight she'd come out with her old high school girlfriend Tia as a way to shut off her brain for a night.

She couldn't get Ty's dark, smoldering stare out of her head. She displeased the hell out of him, so why was that a turn-on?

"Wanna dance?" A cowboy extended a hand, smiling at her from under his battered hat brim.

She shook her head. She had no interest in a cowpoke when men like the Boot Knockers existed. "She might want to dance." She pointed at her girlfriend, who jumped to her feet, throwing Bree an unapologetic grin as she was whirled onto the dance floor.

The song changed and a line dance broke out. Sighing, Bree hunched over her drink and sipped it. Strawberry and alcohol teased her taste buds but she wanted so much more.

She had to get to the Boot Knockers Ranch. Not to find Ty—no, she needed to avoid that tease at all costs. But to find someone who made her insides tingle as much as Ty had that day, and who actually delivered.

She glanced at the wall clock sporting a beer logo. It was late, but maybe slipping in under cover of darkness would work. She understood a bit more about the workings of the ranch now, and surely she could find someone to play with.

Standing, she gathered her itty-bitty jeweled handbag and waved at her friend until she caught her attention. She waved Bree away, laughing and having fun with her dance partner.

Outside Bree welcomed the cooler air on her hot skin. Suddenly she was overheated with the thought of sneaking onto the forbidden ranch. She slipped into her Jeep and headed out of town.

What did the Boot Knockers do on Friday nights? She was about to find out. Grinning, she navigated the roads to the ranch.

The road forked. Left and she'd end up at home, sitting in front of the TV with her father. Right was sexy cowboy heaven.

Or hell. She wanted to jump into the fires of lust and sin with those hot cowboys. She took the right turn. Partway down the dirt road leading to the ranch, she pulled off into the high weeds and parked. She'd walk in.

When she reached the ranch, not many lights greeted her. Maybe Friday nights were spent in the bungalows having mind-blowing sex.

Tonight I'm getting under one of those red roofs.

The walk did nothing to ease the ache between her legs or cool her thoughts. The closer she got, the more worked up she became. She moved through the night, head swinging side to side and heart thumping. If Ty found her, what would he do this time? Take her to the cops?

No matter, she could sweet-talk her way out of any charge. Ty was no match for her, no matter what he said.

As she approached the swimming pool, soft voices reached her. She paused, straining to hear. She poked her head around the corner, drinking in the view of a woman with short hair settled on the side of the pool, legs spread and her knees up around someone's ears. In the darkness, the woman's features were blurred, but her sounds revealed her pleasure.

Bree's nipples tightened into hard gems. Longing burned hot in her, brighter than the moon. She sneaked away and wandered the ranch but didn't run into any more lovers taking their pleasure in the open. And damn if she wasn't half disappointed not to have run into Ty yet.

In fact, it bothered the hell out of her that he was probably snuggled up with another woman, giving her that same smoldering look that had burned into Bree's mind.

There was one unexplored spot on the ranch—the big metal building lured her. The door opened quietly and candles flickered within, pointing her way to a stage.

Her step faltered as she tried to make sense of what she was seeing. A glorious man in a cowboy hat and leather pants, wielding a whip over a woman's flesh. She was tied to a stool, her bare ass reddened by his attentions.

An invisible rope connected to Bree's pussy yanked, and her panties flooded. She clung to the shadows, watching but yearning to participate. This was just the sort of thing she'd come to the ranch to be part of.

Before she knew her own intentions she was leaving a trail of clothes right up to the stage. When she set foot onto the gleaming floor totally nude, the man in leather turned to her, eyes shining.

His gaze raked over her, leaving her feeling more exposed and almost as shaky as she had under Ty's blazing eyes.

"I'm Bree." She held her head high, breasts thrust forward, leg extended to show it off.

He tipped his hat. "Stowe. They call me the Dom from Down Under." She could see why — or hear it, rather. His Australian accent licked her senses. Wetness pooled on her inner thighs.

"Have you ever played before?"

"No." Her word released as a shiver.

"Pick a word, darlin'." His accent seemed to mix with a Texas drawl, making her nerves leap.

"A word?"

"Any word that has importance to you but comes to mind easily."

She searched her mind, feeling like a blank dunce. She dropped her gaze over his chiseled body to the bulge distending black leather. "Longhorn." It was her university's mascot, as well as the cattle her daddy raised.

His mouth quirked at one side but he gave a nod. "Longhorn it is. Take your place, Bree."

She could hardly make her legs move. She looked between several pieces of furniture scattered around the stage. Padded stools, benches, something with pulleys and ropes. And a cross.

She'd heard about such crosses in sex play but had never seen one. She moved toward it as if tugged by one of those ropes. He lashed the kneeling woman two more times then walked across the stage. His steps were slow and measured and his face looked wicked.

"Place your back against the cross."

She did, quaking inside.

"Now stretch your arms onto the X."

While he roped her onto the frame, she watched him. God, he was a beautiful man. Dark-haired, his jaw angular and rough with stubble. A whip tattoo curved around his pec and his biceps bulged as he pulled the ropes restraining her wrists tight.

"Okay, darlin'?"

"Yes." Her voice sounded almost normal, even if she was shaking.

He tied her ankles next. When he lingered in a crouch, nose brushing near her pussy, she cried out.

"Beautiful. Just like that, Bree. Let yourself free to feel and the experience will be richer. I'll keep you safe, but if you get frightened, say longhorn."

She nodded.

He walked away from her. She twisted her head to watch him deliver a few more light blows to the other woman's bare ass. She wore a ball gag and her sounds were muffled, but Bree understood they weren't cries of pain.

Tingling with awareness, she waited. Stowe paced back to her, a short whip with a leather handle in his grip. "We'll start small. Work you up good before I tell you when to release."

"I need it now," she said breathlessly.

"I like my girls eager, but that sort of behavior won't do, Bree. You wait for your Master to make the choice for you."

"No. Please. I came here to get what I need."

He flicked the whip, and short tassels licked over her bare breast. She sucked in a sharp breath, struggling against her bonds. "Hold still," he ordered.

"Use the handle of that whip in my pussy."

"No," he barked.

She hung on the cross, chastised but dripping wet. Too many minutes passed while he returned to the other woman and made her squeal with pleasure. He sucked her nipples, painted her juices over her clit and then did exactly what Bree wanted—he slid the whip handle into the other woman's pussy and fucked her until she grew pink and screamed her release.

Bree watched from hooded eyes, burning, needing what he was giving that woman. Why wasn't he punishing *her*? She wiggled, rattling the cross. Then Stowe turned his attention to her.

* * * * *

When Ty entered the auditorium, he felt the change in the air. Excitement hung there, along with a silence he couldn't wrap his head around. He walked down the center aisle, thinking to take a seat and watch Stowe in action. Since that night he'd fantasized about controlling Bree, he'd become more fascinated with the BDSM life.

He stopped dead.

Long, blonde hair hung around a delicate oval of a face he recognized. Bree. Splayed on the cross, her trim patch of pale curls glistening in the candle flames lighting the stage.

Stowe had the crop and he was spanking her hard, pink nipples.

A roar built in Ty's chest as he stampeded down the aisle. He mounted the stage in one leap, temples pounding with fury. He ripped the crop from Stowe's hand and threw himself in front of the woman who had no goddamn business here.

"Ty!"

"I'll deal with you later," he told Bree a split second before Stowe barreled into him. He rocked Ty's head with a punch to the jaw. Ty felt his jaw creak under the force. Blood filled his mouth, driving his anger.

He threw himself at Stowe, landing an uppercut to the midsection and another to the man's cheek.

"I'll kick your ass for interrupting, Ty. She was in her headspace," Stowe growled.

Jesus, her headspace? No one was putting Bree anywhere unless Ty did it. He launched himself at Stowe, flattening him onto the stage. They struggled, fists flying, boots glancing off shins. Ty took a hit to the left nut that punched the breath from him. But he'd taken worse hits from stronger men, cattle too. He came back twice as strong, giving Stowe a blow that made him curl up like a bug.

Ty scrambled to his feet, spit a glob of blood and grabbed his knife from his pocket. Bree's eyes grew round as he came at her with the blade. He edged it beneath the ropes binding her and cut her down.

"Get your clothes. You're coming with me."

She didn't move. Dammit, was she still in some strange, dreamlike headspace under Stowe's spell? Almost roaring his displeasure, Ty wrapped his fingers around her waist. Her breasts were pink from blows, and her arousal fogged the air.

Stowe was on his feet, glaring. "Don't ever come back to this stage, Ty."

"No problem." He dragged Bree off. Her clothes were spread up the side aisle like breadcrumbs leading into the forbidden forest. Pissed off more than he ever had been in his life, he picked them up and shoved them into her arms. She stared straight ahead, eyes glassy.

Hell, what if she was really hurt? Maybe she needed to be brought back like a hypnosis patient. For several minutes he caressed her bare body, checking her for marks. Her wrists were pink but nothing that needed attention. When she started to pull away from his touch, he locked her against his side and walked her naked ass out of the auditorium.

Outside, she found her voice — and anger.

She whirled on him. "How dare you? You barge in, beat up my Master then cut me off the cross?"

"Your Master," he spat, feeling that deep internal itch in his blood. "Stowe's the Master of many women. You're one in a long line, sweetheart."

She didn't seem to care. "You had no business stopping what we were doing!" She stamped her little foot on the turf, and, damn, that riled him. Heat built in his groin, making his fly strain against his cock.

"Don't test me, woman."

She jogged alongside him, breasts jiggling, driving him mad with the need to pin her against the nearest wall and fuck her silly.

"You can't do what Stowe did to me, so you run in and use your fists to stop it."

He glared at her. "You think I'm less of a man than him?"

"Hell yes. You're nothing like him, nowhere near his caliber of expertise." Blue lightning flashed in her eyes.

They reached his truck and Ty practically threw her inside. She sat there, facing forward, clothes bundled against her nudity. Satisfaction swam in his head. Maybe he'd finally shut her up.

As soon as he climbed behind the wheel, she started again. "Where's your client, Ty? Why aren't you with her?"

"My work is none of your business," he ground out, almost twisting the key off in the ignition. Why did Bree urge him to grind his teeth until they all broke off? He ran his tongue over them. Hell, one of them felt loose after meeting with Stowe's fist.

"You're probably going to say your client is satisfied because you're that good."

He swung his head to look at her. In the darkness, her eyes glittered, her lips were swollen as if she'd bitten them during her play with Stowe.

With a growl, Ty grabbed her and hauled her across the console and into his lap. Soft, sweet curves landed smack on his hard cock.

Her eyes opened so wide a sliver of white appeared around each iris.

"I *am* that good." He kissed her, giving her the harsh rasp of his beard on her skin, marking her. Plunging his tongue into her mouth until she was gasping. When he let her up for air, though, she started talking again.

"You think you can kiss me now? You arrogant assho—"

"Don't you ever call me that." He opened his truck door and flung her facedown over his lap. Her head hung out the door, her calves waved in the air near his face. But her ass was right where he wanted it. He gave her a bare-handed slap that yanked a blood-curdling scream from her.

"You like being a bad girl, but I won't allow it. Not on this ranch. I'm going to teach you a lesson." He spanked her again, warming the other cheek. She cried out, fighting like a crazy woman, even as goose bumps broke out on her skin.

"You're not getting away. This is what you want, Bree. Admit it to yourself because I figured it out long ago." He delivered four more slaps to each ass cheek. Her screams turned to whimpers and finally pants.

He rubbed a circle over one hot cheek. God, he wanted to plunge into the shadow between her thighs and make her beg. She hung over his lap, hair dangling around her face.

"What I wouldn't give to see your face." He massaged the other cheek. He couldn't push her too far or harm her. But if she sassed him again, he wouldn't let her get away with it.

He let his fingers travel over her flesh, under the curve, close to her weeping pussy. His mouth watered.

Suddenly she squirmed. He held on to her. "You're not going to live this down, Ty. I'm going to—"

"What? Tell Daddy? I bet he holds a parade in my honor when he finds out I finally spanked your ass."

"Shut up!"

"Give me a safe word. Now."

"No. You don't deserve it."

"You don't like this then? You don't want this?"

There was a beat of silence. Then she rasped, "Longhorn."

"Oh, baby girl. Why do you misbehave?" Throbbing with need, he spanked her again. Right cheek, left. Each crack fueled something primal in him, and he knew there was no going back. They either killed each other or fell into bed for the biggest, longest, hottest satisfaction of their lives.

* * * * *

As each vibration of Ty's hand on her ass rocketed through her system, she bit back a cry. This was so much more intense than what she'd experienced while Stowe spanked her nipples with the crop.

No, Ty's hand felt unbearably intimate, and his words set fire to her.

Did she want this? More than anything. But how could she? It was so confusing. She kicked at him. One broad palm pinned her spine as he brought his other hand flat on her ass. The sting echoed through her veins. A quiet moan left her—the sound more a reflection of her need than any pain. God, was she finally getting what she'd been looking for?

He spanked her more lightly—several times on each buttock. For a moment she hung there, exposed, aching, aroused as hell.

His breathing was labored, and, judging by the huge bulge against her legs, he was as turned on as she was. She parted her thighs ever so slightly.

"You want me to touch you here?" Without warning he slid his fingers over her soaking folds from bottom to top. He circled her clit then drew his fingers down again. He let them linger near her entrance but didn't plunge them inside. She wiggled backward.

"Do you want this, baby girl?"

Did she? Shit, she was confused. Her body hummed with need, and the feel of his hand and his command of her body had twisted her all up. She didn't even like Ty, did she?

He grazed the übersensitive space between her ass and pussy. She cried out.

"Your body says yes. But I need the words from you."

Seconds ticked by while blood rushed into her head from hanging upside down. Night insects raised a chorus.

She could tell him no and he'd take her home. Maybe if she threatened to tell Daddy about the spanking Ty would just drop her at the border between properties and not tell her father what she'd been doing.

But if she walked away now, she'd never know the pleasure Ty's voice promised.

She struggled to right herself. She wasn't agreeing to anything while dangling over his lap.

He hauled her upright with no effort. She sat on his lap, too close, too aware of her nudity and that blazing look that was back on his face.

"Why do you want me?" she heard herself ask.

Something flickered in his eyes. "Because you need someone to make you behave and the fact that I know I can is just what I need too."

"You think a few smacks on the behind will keep me from coming back to the ranch?"

His lips tightened, turning her inside out. She wanted those hard lips on hers, on her breasts and between her legs. "I plan to show you who's in charge, Bree. And to give you what you need." He skimmed a fingertip over her nipple, strumming it along with every nerve ending in her body.

"What do I need?"

His eyes lit up as if someone had switched on a bulb. "I'll show you. Give your consent."

She stared into his eyes, burning up with the fierce need she saw there.

"I'll take you someplace where it's just the two of us."

Her body screamed, *Yes, finally!* But what happened afterward? And what if this was only a trick to ditch her?

She stared at his mouth for an eternal heartbeat.

He made a noise deep in his chest that made her gaze flash to his. Their stares held. "Yes," she whispered.

He kissed her — taking her lips and tongue with a possession she'd never known. Shuddering, she wrapped her arms around him and gave him the lead. Power thrummed beneath his muscles.

He flipped his tongue against hers, and they shared a moan. He tasted like cinnamon gum and something earthy she couldn't get close enough to. She wiggled restlessly and his cock hardened further.

While they kissed he plucked at her nipples with calloused fingers. Had her breasts ever been this sensitive before? She felt as if the switch that had turned the lights on in his eyes also powered her body. She arched into his touch.

"Baby girl." It shouldn't be so damn erotic when he called her that, but it was. He scooped a hand under her thigh, bringing her closer. "I have to drive. That means I need you in the passenger's seat."

"Wh-where are we going?"

"Someplace where I can make you scream with ecstasy until your throat's raw." With that, he lifted her over the console and placed her on the seat. She settled back to watch him, drinking in his hard profile. Straight nose, strong jaw. It was stubbled and not clean-shaven. His eyes hooded.

When he shifted the truck into gear, the moonlight caught the hairs on his arms and accentuated the muscles. She shivered again.

He didn't look at her, just drove. They bounced across the field and clattered over a wooden bridge spanning a shallow creek. In rainy times, the creek would swell and probably swallow the bridge. She didn't ask where they were going.

It was hard to draw a normal breath. She was nude in a man's truck, giving him control of her body and needs.

"You aren't tricking me, are you? Taking me home?"

He sent her a look that raised steam from her. "Long way around, isn't it?"

She lifted her jaw. "Why should I trust you?"

A muscle in the crease of his jaw leaped. "Because I'm going to give you exactly what you want."

"How do you know what I want?" Irritation grew, his kisses too distant now that they were away from the ranch and she wasn't in his lap.

He stopped the truck. Put it in Park. When he turned to her, her heart slammed into her ribs. Before he could speak, she rattled off, "Are you going to tell me you've met dozens of women like me and satisfied all their needs?"

He gave a slight shake of his head, almost as if confused. "No, because I haven't. But that doesn't stop me from knowing what *you* need, baby girl."

"Stop calling me that."

"Do you prefer sugar tits?"

"No!" Her damn traitorous nipples hardened as if his words had summoned them to peak. She folded her arms over her breasts but he only eyed them more wolfishly.

"I'll call you baby girl because it fits you."

Her stomach did a loop-the-loop.

He caught a tendril of her hair, gaze flaying her open, exposing parts of her she didn't know she had. Her mind tumbled with emotions and her breaths came faster.

"I'm not childish."

"No, but you like being a brat. And I'm here to tell you...you won't get away with it. Not with me."

Her mouth fell open.

He got out of the truck and came around to her door. She sat there, torn. Frightened. Alive. Needy as hell. And she wanted more of his kisses. But something else had risen in her—and it felt strangely like an electric current when they looked at each other.

She climbed out into the moonlight, clothes abandoned on the truck floor. He captured her ass in his hands, reminding her of the ache he'd raised. "Ow, I'm sore!"

"You're not sore enough and you know it."

Her pussy squeezed. Juices soaked her inner thighs.

"Turn around and put your hands on the truck."

His dark tone slithered through her, spearing her with need.

"I'm not sure I want to be at your mercy. Not sure you can handle the job."

"Bree." His voice was a warning.

Her clit throbbed. Something about taunting him really pulled the trigger for her. She wanted to drive him crazy.

She pushed harder. "I'm going back to finish what I started with Stowe."

"Like hell." His eyes flashed. He whirled her, pressing her against the metal still holding the heat of the day. He reached past her and into the truck. She shook at the sight of rope — both with trepidation and desire. When he looped it around her ankles, she grabbed his head and tried to guide him where she wanted him most.

He slapped her ass — hard. She screamed. Nipples burning from being so tight, her inner walls shaking under the pressure building inside her, she found herself truly at his mercy. But she had no desire to use her safe word.

He tied her ankles together then bound her hands behind her back. As he gained his feet, he let his hard chest slide over her stinging ass and up her body. She trembled, mind spinning with the force of her desire.

"You're lucky no one can see you out here."

She twisted her head to try to see him. If she could just look at his face, she'd know if she'd pushed him far enough. His voice gave nothing away. "Maybe I'd ask them to spank me."

"No." His tone was dead, but his mouth on her throat was not. She gasped as he sucked hard enough to leave a love bite. She squirmed closer even as she tried to get away.

"So far you haven't given me…" *pant, pant,* "…any pleasure."

He curled a finger over her clit. She bucked, crying out as need crashed over her. Red-hot lust seared her core, but he removed his finger.

"You jerk," she whimpered.

He bit into her shoulder, depressing the skin lightly, but it was enough to stimulate her beyond reason. Her pulse thundered and the throbbing in her pussy increased. "Call me that again and you'll pay," he rumbled.

Was he baiting her? Of course she wasn't going to pass up the opportunity to speak her mind. "You've been an incredible asshole, tearing me away from pleasure. First with Elliot, then that other guy — twice! And Stowe..." She drowned in memories of Stowe's crop on her nipples and the dark, promising look in his eyes.

"They aren't going to lay a hand on you unless I tell them to."

She shuddered. Would he do that? Invite other men to touch her? Her chest rose and fell.

"I can see that works you up. But don't think you're going to get away with calling me an asshole." He spanked her with rapid taps that jarred her from head to toe and pussy to nipple. She stopped crying out after only a few taps, swallowed by calm.

At least until he thrust two fingers into her pussy. She splintered, coming with such force her knees buckled. As she pulsated, he supported her against the truck, kissing her neck, whispering.

The orgasm flooded her with a warmth she'd never known.

Ty's mouth was at her ear. "That's it, baby girl. Come for me. Be nice and I'll give you anything you want."

She nodded, pushing back against his fingers, wanting more.

"So beautiful. Your spirit is what every man wishes he could tame, but only I can. Do you hear what I'm saying?"

"Uhh." She wanted him to turn her into his arms and kiss her as she still buzzed from the insane orgasm he'd provoked with barely a touch.

If he could do that to her so easily, what would happen if he really took her? Laid her down and thrust into her while kissing her into a melted puddle?

She sagged against him.

"Have you learned your lesson for the night?"

"Yes. Please."

"Will you call me any more names?"

She might if he didn't give her what she wanted. But her demands hadn't worked with Stowe, and Ty seemed more in control than that leather-clad man.

She shook her head.

"Good girl." He turned her. When she met his gaze, deep emotion rushed upward, choking her. She needed his kisses.

Stretching onto tiptoe, she upturned her face. He cradled her jaw and kissed her, long and sweet, sending surges of warmth into new parts. Small noises escaped her. Before she'd drunk her fill of his manly flavors, he pulled away.

He crouched and untied her ankles. The hemp had prickled into her skin, but he rubbed the bands of irritation above each foot. Her breath caught as he skimmed his hands up each calf, tracing the lines to knees, inner thighs. Using a finger on each pussy lip, he spread her.

Gulping for air, she watched him lean close. Hot breath, hotter tongue. She cried out as he lapped a figure eight around her clit.

"Who are you hot for, Bree?"

"Y-you." She wished her hands were loose to feel his hair. She looped her bound hands around his neck. The urge to yank him in and take what she wanted was suppressed as their gazes locked.

"That's right," he drawled before snaking his tongue into her wet folds.

* * * * *

Hell, he could listen to her sweet sounds of surrender all night. He intended to. Ty forced her to hold his stare while tasting every inch of her soaking pussy. Juices coated his tongue, the sweetest candy. His cock couldn't get harder.

But her eyes…they were wide, tender as he unraveled her bit by bit. Something told him this couldn't be a one-time occurrence. He'd need more.

Reaching around her, he slicked a finger between her legs, gathering her cream. As he spread her wetness over her ass, she cried out.

"Don't close your eyes. Look right at the man pleasuring you."

She brought her gaze back, trusting him with it—the windows to her soul.

It didn't surprise him that he wanted to own her for tonight. She'd been under his skin far too many weeks to not claim everything. He drove his tongue into her sweet channel, using his upper lip to chafe her hard clit. She flooded his tongue, and he rewarded her by easing a fingertip into the tight seam of her ass.

She didn't open to him immediately, revealing she was untouched there.

"This is mine first."

"Mmm." She had gone incoherent, but her eyes spoke loudly. They were wide, begging.

He teased her with a fingertip, gathering more wetness, then moved to her nether hole, trying to loosen her to allow him to glide a finger inside. He trailed his tongue through her wetness, enamored with her flavors and the power she handed him.

Even the way her bound hands rested against his neck made him feel heady. Drunk.

"Loosen up for me. Give me entrance," he rumbled against her clit.

She cried out, her pussy flexing under his lips. She was close. But he wanted to extend her pleasure and introduce her to something more. That's what she was here for, after all. And he'd be damned if another Boot Knocker had a chance to do this first.

Visions of her with Stowe blinded him for a minute, and he growled, driving his tongue deep. She spread her legs wide, shaking as he fucked her wildly with his mouth. Short gasps erupted from her.

And he took advantage, sinking a fingertip past the tight ring of muscle. He wanted to stretch her enough that when he took her over the edge of bliss, she remembered him for a long time. The sting on her backside would keep her wondering what else she was missing.

He pushed deeper—with tongue and finger. When he felt her resistance give way, he slid his finger in another fraction. He didn't want to hurt her, but she sounded far from injured. And she was wet enough to provide good lubrication.

His own ass burned. What he wouldn't give for a cock in his ass right now as he licked his naughty girl.

"Ty!"

"Hmm?"

"Stop teasing me."

He backed off immediately. Sitting back on his heels, he stared into her eyes, letting her see his displeasure.

"I...I'm sorry." Her voice faltered.

"Don't be sorry. Be *patient*. You won't get your way with demands."

She nodded, her body seeming to glisten under the moon.

He licked his lips slowly. "You taste so damn good."

"Finish what you started then."

An irritated sigh left him as he gained his feet. Grabbing the rope looping her hands together, he began to walk with her. Towing her behind him, his body sparking with desire. She was so bad—and so good. He needed to reach inside her and make her see—

See what? He didn't have a clue what the fuck he was doing. He was running on pure instinct, adrenaline and raw need.

The trapper's cabin wasn't far along the creek. It might have a few cobwebs but it also had a cot. He intended to tie Bree to it and torment her until she gave up total control to him. He'd almost had her—then she'd opened her damn sassy mouth and gotten greedy again.

"Where are we?" Her voice was a shiver on the breeze.

"The place where you're going to give yourself to me." He threw her a look. "All of you."

She made a noise sounding close to a squeak but allowed him to pull her inside the cabin without resistance. She moved her wrists.

"Do the ropes hurt?"

"A little."

"You like that hurt, don't you?"

She panted. "A little."

Holding her gaze, he shut the door, enclosing them in a dark cocoon. He could see enough through the small window to tell she still wore that sweet, begging look.

He yanked off his shirt, unbuckled his belt and unzipped his fly. When he pushed the denim and cotton down his hips, his cock sprang free. Hard, snaked with veins, glistening at the tip.

"Time to make me happy, Bree. Take me in your mouth. Every inch. And then I'll reward you."

Her eyes widened. "I don't know if I can."

"Can you try?"

"Yes." She was breathless. She sank to her knees, hands roped before her. When his cock skimmed her lips, he thought he'd die. Dark need radiated up from his balls, and he wanted nothing more than to sink into her mouth hard and fast.

But no. He had to give her the chance to please him.

As he watched his cock disappear into the warm haven of her mouth, he smoothed his hands over her silky hair. "That's it, baby girl. You can fit it all, I know you can."

She moaned around him, juddering his length. Precome dripped from his tip.

"Deeper. You can do it. Use your tongue. Jesus. Hell yessss." He couldn't look away if he wanted. She was taking him like a fucking pro. When he reached her soft palate in the back of her throat, she flicked her eyes up at him, panic there.

"More," he grated out.

She mewled.

He caressed the delicate shell of her ear, down to her jaw. "Tip your head and take me."

She angled her head up, eyes wide and glassy. Stowe said she'd been in her headspace? Fuck, Stowe didn't know shit about headspace. Bree was almost there, though. She wanted to please Ty so she could get the pleasure only he could provide.

He sank into her throat, his balls kissing her chin. For two heartbeats, their gazes held.

He rocked back, pulling his length free of her mouth. Saliva strung them together, and she licked her lips.

"Get on the bed, gorgeous." He devoured the look of her, imprinting it on his memory. His heart was a wild horse stampeding faster with each passing moment. He'd never been so riled before, and he had no idea where this would end, but it wasn't going to be tonight.

He had Bree "Spitfire" Roberts naked and quivering with need for him.

He pressed her onto her back and spread her legs wide. "Do I need to tie them apart?"

"No."

"What if I want to?"

"I—"

He waited for some smart-ass retort, but she released a quivering sigh.

"If you want to, tie me."

Nice and compliant. *Good girl.* He kicked off his boots and stripped away the rest of his clothing. His cock was an arrow pointing his way home to the shadow between her thighs.

"I want—" She broke off, holding her hands up.

"You're allowed to ask for things but not demand. Not with me, Bree. You understand?"

Her breasts jiggled under her laboring breaths. "Will you untie my hands so I can touch you?"

Fuck yes. He tugged the knot free and rubbed the rope chafes. When she put her hands on his chest, he thought he'd burn up. Her scorching touch filled him with something deep and aching and beautiful.

He found a condom and handed it to her. "Put that on me."

With a noise of want, she sat up and worked the rubber over his length. When her gaze flicked up to his again, he cupped her chin and kissed her. Plundering her mouth as he lay her down and poised at the quick of her.

"Ty!"

"That's it. Say my name because I want you to know whom you belong to tonight."

"Ty, please."

He burrowed the head of his cock between her plump lips, dying with primal need. "Look into my eyes. Don't look away."

"I won't."

He sank deep. She clenched around him immediately. He clung to the edge of control, driving into her again and again, hitching her thigh up to reach deeper. She hugged his every inch so perfectly. So hot, so sweet when she wasn't giving him lip. And even when she was, he liked her too damn much.

"Hold on to me," he rasped. Lifting her off the bed, he plowed into her, driven by some unseen force. She threw her arms around him and kissed him. When her sharp teeth broke the skin on his lower lip, he exploded.

She came with him, clamping around his cock until he grew dizzy. In a burst, he breathed again, spurting two times, three, four. She rocked her hips upward, milking him.

"Holy—" he roared.

"Fuck," she finished.

They collapsed onto the bed.

Chapter Six

With Ty's rough fingers blazing trails over and over Bree's skin and his hard body glued to hers, she tried to make sense of what just happened.

He'd given her the best release of her life. But she'd been sex deprived for a while. Or it could have something to do with Stowe working her up first.

Or the way Ty commanded every part of me.

She felt him inside her head still, and she didn't know if she liked him there. He'd torn down walls she hadn't known existed. Making her hold his gaze, take his cock into her throat...

In the end she'd gotten him back a little, though. A bead of blood shimmered on his lower lip. He licked it off and gave her a warning look. "Don't think you won't pay for that."

"You liked it."

He rolled onto his knees then disappeared into the little bathroom. She watched his carved ass move away. When he returned, she admired his front more.

"What's that look all about, huh, baby girl?" He hovered over her and stole her breath with his beauty. Arms rigid, brown hair tumbling into his blazing eyes. He shook it away. "I like you coming apart for me. And I did make a promise to claim your ass."

Her stomach hollowed out, even as her pussy spasmed. "No you didn't."

"Maybe I only made the promise in my head. Either way. Roll over."

When she didn't move, his eyes glittered. "Not so brave, are you, baby girl?"

Oh hell no. He wasn't calling her a coward, especially when it came to sex. She was more adventurous than any man had ever been able to live up to. She flopped onto her stomach. Her ass cheeks felt hot still. Were they red? A thrill traveled through her.

Ty grabbed a pillow and wadded it under her, hitching her ass higher into the air. Apprehension jolted her. What was he going to do? She grew wetter with every sweet tick of the minutes.

When he clamped his hands around her globes, she cried out.

"You sore?"

"You don't have to sound so damn happy about it."

"Oh, but I am. You can't imagine the pleasure I get from spanking you."

"You're sick."

He pinched one cheek and she reared. "Ow!"

"Stay down, stay still if you know what's good for you."

"You're twisted, getting off on controlling me."

"Damn straight. So are you. Otherwise why would you be so—" he eased his fingers into her pussy, "—fucking—" deeper, "—wet?"

She was. Drenched, gagging for this harsh play she found more arousing than anything in the world. She pushed backward, taking his fingers to the knuckles.

He fucked her pussy, making her writhe, the juicy noises clogging the air. When she started to squeak with impending release, he withdrew his fingers and painted the wetness over her pucker.

She tensed, heart pounding. The feel of him touching her there earlier still lingered. It drove her crazy. She bucked upward and met something soft and wet.

Mother of pearl, it's his tongue.

Burrowing her face in the clean-smelling blankets, she lost herself to the taboo tonguing he was giving her ass. He ran the tip around every ridge, circling until she was rising off the bed to the rhythm he set. He teased the opening, parting her with his tongue then backing off.

She fisted the covers and begged with her body. Knowing he'd stop if she demanded more. Maybe if she begged nicely he'd give her what she really wanted. In some sick way, she'd be giving him something in turn—he obviously got off on having her at his mercy.

"Ty, please? Please make me come."

He rumbled, and her heart hitched. She was right. He was actually fulfilling a need in him too. She gasped as he sank his tongue and wiggled it. Deep but not enough. She wanted his fingers and later his cock stretching her backside.

She wanted him to give up some control to her too, losing himself in this forbidden and exciting game.

"Ty, please. Give it to me."

He slapped her ass, making her jerk—and flood with arousal. "Give you what?"

"Give me release."

"Ask nice, baby girl."

"Can I have it, please?"

He tongued her ass, making her cry out. When he slipped his fingers under her and stroked the hard knot of nerves on her pussy, she drifted. Quaking, stomach muscles jumping, losing herself to pleasure. She climbed and climbed.

Another finger speared her pussy and one drove into her ass. She burst, floating, seeing stars.

His name was on her lips all night long.

* * * * *

Dawn streamed through the small window and trickled over Bree's soft body. Every dip and swell was light and shadow, a map he wanted to navigate with his hands and tongue.

She tugged his hair and a few strands broke free. *Insolent little brat.*

He dived for her throat, biting it until she writhed. Her heels struck his legs as she

149

kicked. He threw his thigh over both of hers, pinning her. His cock jutted into her hip and damn if the woman didn't purposely rub against it.

"Let me go! Stop biting me! I'm going to have a mark."

He released her then delivered a long, slow lick from collarbone to ear. "You like it. You'll go home and look in the mirror at the mark I left and get hot for me all over again."

"Humble, I see."

"I know women."

"I'm not just any woman."

"I know *you*."

She fell still, relaxing in his hold. He snuggled closer, nose skimming her fragrant shoulder. After a few minutes, he asked, "What do you want to do when you grow up?"

She swung her face to pierce him with her bright stare. "I am grown up."

"It was an expression. I know you are."

Instead of answering, she closed her eyes. But her breathing didn't deepen as it would if she were sleepy. No, she was doing an internal search for the answer. More minutes passed.

"My mother wanted me to be a professor," he said.

Her eyes popped open and she looked at him. "Yeah? Professor of what?" Her hand swished back and forth over his spine, bringing him extreme peace. He cuddled her closer.

"University professor. Teaching business and marketing, I guess."

"Hmm. Bet she finally realized you weren't smart enough."

He pinched her bottom hard. She bucked and squealed until he caressed the spot then lower under the curve of her ass. A stuttering sigh escaped her and she grew soft in his arms again.

"I was valedictorian of my class," he said.

"Impressive. Brains and brawn. Why did you decide to go with the brawn for a career?"

"Maybe I'm a little like you, using my looks before they fade."

"Then you'll build up that character? Good luck with that."

He snorted. "I know you want me to spank you for that remark, but I'm not giving you what you want this time. We're having a talk."

Her fingers swished over his skin, back and forth, slower with each pass. Maybe she was growing sleepy after all. Extreme tenderness welled inside him.

"I'm a Boot Knocker because of a bet I made."

"With whom?"

"Aw, you used the correct pronoun. See? And you think you're just a pretty face."

She grabbed his hand, raised it to her mouth and bit it. Laughing, he pinned her more firmly. "A bet with myself. I had the opportunity to come here. I'd interviewed with Hugh and he'd given me a great offer. Free housing, meals. Guaranteed fun. And a retirement package as well as the fresh air I craved."

"Sounds like a no-brainer."

"Right. Except my mom wanted that professor in the family. Secretly I think she had a crush on some professor in her time and thought highly of the career. I was faced with a choice—make her dreams come true or sow my wild oats while I could."

"Doesn't sound like a hard decision to me. Who the hell would choose teaching over having lots of sex?"

He continued, ignoring her. Holding up his forearm sporting the tattoo, he said, "I'm better than average at poker. But some of it is chance. I figured if I turned over a winning card, I'd be a Boot Knocker. If I lost, I was going on to get my doctorate so I could teach."

"And you won." Her eyes were jewels, brighter blue in the dim lighting. She brought his forearm down until her lips crushed against the inky lines of his tattoo.

"I bet you're glad I'm here," he rumbled.

"Nope."

He dug his cock into the soaking flesh between her thighs. "Want to say that again?"

"Maybe I have a thing for professors too."

He delivered a slap to her outer thigh that resounded, and she sucked in a sharp gasp. Then she went crazy, fighting him, and he made her give in with long sweeps of his tongue over hers. In the end, she conceded defeat—she admitted she was pretty damn happy he was a Boot Knocker who knew his way around a woman's body.

* * * * *

"Ty, catch that rope for me, would ya?" Riggs's words didn't register. Ty stared at him until Riggs waved a hand. "Earth to Ty. The rope."

He jolted and caught the rope dangling from the hayloft. Ty's feet were firmly planted on the barn floor, but he felt as if he were still circling the sun.

Riggs laughed. "What the hell's up with you?"

"Nothin'." He wasn't going to admit that Bree had wheedled her way into his brain—not even to himself. No, not wheedled—consumed his every thought. In the two days since he'd taken her in the trapper's cabin, he couldn't get her out of his head.

Thank God he had a week off now.

"All right, Mr. Nothin's Wrong, tie that rope to the damn motor so I can hoist it into the loft." Riggs yanked the rope and it slipped from Ty's hands. Like a crazy cat, Ty made a snag for it, but Riggs ripped it out of reach again.

"Glad you're enjoying yourself, Riggs." He pushed his hat back to see his friend better. Riggs cocked a grin and let the rope fall into

Ty's hand. He drew it down to bind around a small engine. They didn't need the engine right now, but that didn't mean the ranch wanted to get rid of it. Storing it in the loft was the best idea. There were other odds and ends up there, waiting for a rainy day when they'd become useful again.

He watched the engine sway a few feet off the ground and begin its ascent into the loft, but his mind was miles away, back in the trapper's cabin. After Bree's first orgasm, he'd flipped her over and gathered her close. Driving into her again and again while holding her gaze had made him realize a lot.

First, she'd never be fulfilled with the kind of sex she was seeking. Meaningless physical release wasn't what she wanted, even if she thought she did.

Second, he was frightened by how explosive their sex was.

He'd thrown out all restraint and pounded into her hard. When she splintered around him, his roar had shaken the walls of the cabin. For several minutes after he pumped out countless spurts of come, he'd drifted.

Never done that before.

After he'd collapsed on the bed beside her, she'd curled up with a thigh over his, her light caresses still zinging through his memory. Before the sky had fully lightened, he'd led her back to the truck and watched her dress. Without a word he'd returned her to her car parked along the lane. Even when he took her cell and plugged his number into it, they didn't speak.

But he'd kissed her until she squeaked for more. Then he put her into the car and watched her drive off in a cloud of dust.

"What the hell's the matter with you, Ty?" Riggs's voice jerked him from his musings.

He realized the engine was safely in the loft above and Riggs was descending the ladder like a well-practiced high diver. Ty shook himself. "Nothin'."

"A lot of nothin'. C'mon. We've got work to do." Riggs hit the floor and shot off to the barn door. Ty followed his lead for the rest of the day, throwing himself into backbreaking labor that never quite wiped his mind clean.

Was Bree thinking about him as much as he was her? If she wasn't, he'd spank her ass. He could nearly feel the heat radiating from her skin after his attentions. His cock was hardening.

He thrust the pitchfork into the hay pile.

"Never knew you to be so quiet." Riggs eyed him. The man's dark eyes could draw secrets from the most closemouthed man. But Ty couldn't confide in Riggs. He was one of his bosses and Hugh's lover. From what he'd heard, Boot Knockers who were found to be unfocused had bigger issues once they faced Hugh.

"Just tired I guess."

"Good thing it's your week off then." Riggs's muscles gleamed with sweat as he pitched fresh hay into a muddy area of the paddock.

"It is." Good thing because Ty couldn't dream of pleasuring any woman besides the one in his head at the moment. Bree had a tight grip on him, and that had to stop. The only way to evict her from his thoughts was to sate himself with her. He'd text her later and ask her to come to the ranch.

"You've been seeing a lot of Elliot," Riggs said.

Ty looked up, trying to process his words. "Oh? Yeah." *Fork, pitch. Fork, pitch.*

"He was a little broken up about Jack leaving the ranks." Jack had inspired a lot of lust in several of the guys. When he'd finally settled on Paul and Lissy, he'd been missed.

"Are you saying he's latched on to me now?" Ty had spent enough time thinking about Elliot's soft looks to realize everyone else must have noticed as well.

"Has he?"

"I dunno." He dug in again.

"Do you feel a connection to him?"

Agitation washed over Ty. He scooped hay faster. "He's got a nice cock and gives great head."

"There's no need to get defensive. I was just wondering if you were feeling the same things Elliot is."

Ty looked up. "Has he talked to you?"

Riggs didn't need to say so. His expression revealed it all.

"He has."

Riggs nodded.

"What's he said?"

"Only that he thinks about you all the time and he wants to understand you better. You seem hot and cold to him."

Ty looked at his boots. Hot and cold? Hell yeah. Ty didn't want any relationships. In fact, Ms. Bree had no place in his head either.

"I can see you're conflicted."

Shit, could Riggs detect his confusion over Bree? He wasn't doing a very good job at maintaining his professional distance, apparently. He wanted nothing more than to keep Bree in his bed all week and Elliot had gotten the wrong signals. How?

"Hugh was conflicted too, you know." Riggs's voice grew a little wistful.

Snapping his head up, he said, "This isn't you and Hugh all over again."

"No?"

"No." He stared into his friend's eyes for a long heartbeat.

"Is it Jack and Paul then?"

"Do you mean that I'm like Paul, resisting what I feel for another man?"

Riggs gave a nod.

"No. I mean, I like Elliot. He's a good friend and we have a good time together. But am I in love with him? No."

"Could you be?"

"What's with the interrogation? Has Elliot asked you to feel me out?"

"Not at all," he said immediately. "I guess I have a soft spot for guys who find themselves longing for someone they can't have. The way Elliot's wanting you."

"We're fuck buddies and far from exclusive."

"If you're with him often enough, he might misunderstand your intentions."

Shit, this was exactly the reason Ty didn't want to become bogged down in some relationship. He couldn't deal with emotional games. But he didn't want to hurt Elliot either. He pushed out a breath through his nose and leaned on his pitchfork.

"We've only fucked a couple times this month. I think he's been with Jeremy more."

"So you've thought about the situation." Riggs returned to pitching hay.

"Maybe I need to avoid him." Ty gazed out at the field where a few horses grazed. He and Elliot were friends and the thought of never spending time with him again created a pinching sensation in his chest. He loved sleeping with men—taking them hard and rough where he couldn't do that as much with a woman without hurting her.

And he wasn't against falling in love with a man. But not yet and not Elliot. How many times did he need to tell everyone it was casual sex? Lots of Boot Knockers slept with Elliot. He didn't like the thought of avoiding him, but he would if necessary.

"Think about it. You have all the time in the world. But I only told you because I want you to be conscious of how you treat Elliot. It matters."

Ty could see it had mattered a lot to Riggs how Hugh had acted with him, and this interference was a reflection of that. Ty nodded. "Will do."

After busting his ass for another two hours alongside Riggs, Ty grabbed a hamburger from the grub house and made off for the shower. Between thinking of Bree and Elliot all day long, he needed some cold water.

The long room filled with cots was empty. All the others were busy with their clients of the week. Ty's shirt clung to his skin, and he stripped it off as he walked the center aisle to his bunk. Bree hadn't returned his shirt. Would she try?

He removed his cell from his back pocket and stared at the screen. No texts, no calls. Bree wasn't pining for him, then. He didn't know whether to feel relieved or pissed off. Deep down he had a feeling she was ignoring him to get a rise from him.

It was working.

Chapter Seven

Bree sat rigidly in the saddle, staring down upon the Boot Knockers Ranch. The moon was bright, shedding enough light for Royal to walk over the ridge and into forbidden territory.

Ty didn't know she was coming. She hadn't known she was going after him until she was in the saddle and halfway to the neighboring property. She needed more from him.

She wasn't finished experimenting, and so far he'd given her more than the others. Even if he hadn't pulled her away from the other Boot Knockers, she had a feeling they couldn't give her what she needed deep down.

Ty had.

Not only searing orgasms but he'd unlocked something. She had no idea how he'd tapped into it or why she needed to open this dark place inside her, and for that reason she was going to find him.

For two days she'd waited for a text summoning her to him. When none came, she got surlier with her father. He'd walked away shaking his head, shoulders slumped. And all of a sudden she'd realized how her words affected him. Ty wouldn't let her get away with it.

A shiver coursed through her. She made a soft clicking noise to Royal and the horse started over the ridge. As the animal picked the best footing, Bree rolled in the saddle. She'd given herself a few orgasms in the days since Ty had his hands on her, but they had only whet her appetite.

The pressure inside her mounted with every step toward the ranch. Where was Ty at this time of night?

She reined up, heart somersaulting. He was probably with a client. Crap, she should have texted him first.

Royal carried her onto the ranch where Bree dismounted and hobbled her horse near the paddock. No one would notice another horse in the darkness.

Drawing a deep breath of the grass-scented air, she hurried to the bunkhouse. Too well she imagined Ty there, stretched facedown on his bunk, his broad back tapering to his carved ass.

What would he do when he found her on the ranch again?

Slap my ass.

The quivers of need increased. On light feet, she ran across the grounds. The bunkhouse door opened silently, and she peered inside. Moonlight slanted through a few windows, but Ty's bunk was swallowed by darkness.

Most of the guys would be with their women in the bungalows. Only the guys who were off duty for the week would be sleeping here, unless they got lucky and were asked for a threesome. She hoped Ty was in bed.

Heart thundering in her ears, she tiptoed forward, noting the rest of the bunks were empty. The closer she got, the wetter she became. He'd given her such pleasure her body craved more. And that ache he'd created while fingering her ass had only escalated in the past few days. He'd claimed her in that way, and he was damn well keeping his promise to finish the job.

She drew up short. Ty was there as she'd hoped, lying on his side, a muscled arm slung over his eyes. In the dim light, she caught sight of dark hairs shadowing his jaw.

Her stomach plunged. Excitement tingled in her fingertips. What would he do to her when she slid into bed with him?

She had to find out.

At his bedside, she removed her jeans and flannel shirt. Wearing only panties, she crowded onto the narrow mattress with the man who had blown her mind — for the first time in her life.

That's why she needed to see him again. It had nothing to do with a burning need in her chest. He was just another Boot Knocker.

One who makes me dripping wet.

His body was as hard as steel but steaming hot. She gasped as her flesh met his.

In a blink he came awake, bolting upright, nearly sending her crashing to the floor. He caught her hip, yanking her into his side.

"Dammit, Bree." Groggy words passed his full lips.

"Sorry. I didn't know who you were until I was in bed with you," she lied, hoping to rouse him.

He went dead still, each tightening of muscle lighting a new fire along her nerves. She clenched her thighs together, holding in that delicious ache.

"What the hell do you mean you didn't know who you were crawling into bed with?" His tone echoed with danger.

"I didn't know."

He gripped her hips hard, the bite of his fingers oh-so good. She panted. "You'd damn well better backtrack, baby girl, because I'm like an angry bear when someone wakes me."

She wanted to cuddle closer to him. What was it about the lines he kept drawing that made her want to dash through them? And he almost seemed to taunt her, urging her to ignore his authority.

Running a hand up his ridged side, she searched his face. The hard planes thrilled her. "I wasn't sure I'd find you here."

"So you thought you'd climb naked into bed with any old cowboy?" He locked his hands on her breasts, the viselike touch rocking her.

She moaned. "Any old cowboy would love to have me wrapped around him. I'd hoped to find someone willing to claim me." She grabbed his wrist and moved his hand along her torso around to her ass. "Here."

"Like hell. This is mine." He flipped her onto her stomach and pinned her with his weight, cock grinding into her ass as he fumbled with the sides of her panties. In a second he had her stripped. The first spank caught her off guard.

Crying out, she rode out the pleasure-pain. He smacked her again, her hands locked in one of his. He placed his mouth to her ear and rumbled, "You're playing with fire, baby girl."

God yes, and she loved every minute.

"Disregarding my rules."

"You don't rule me," she shot out then held her breath. Waiting for the punishment.

He didn't disappoint. He reared back and pulled her hips off the mattress. He spanked her right cheek until it felt hot and swollen. Then he turned to the left. Her pussy flooded, juices trickling down her inner thigh. She buried her face in the pillow that smelled like him and drowned in a sea of want.

"By the time I'm done with you tonight, you'll know your place."

"I belong down here."

"Like…" *spank,* "…hell. Now tell me where you belong."

"If you think I'm going to say I belong at home, alone on a ranch with my father and old ranch hands, you're wrong."

He plastered his bare body to hers, scorching her spine. Grunting, she pushed back. "I didn't say that, though you're right. You shouldn't be here, but I'm going to show you where you belong." With a nip to her earlobe that made her cry out, he probed her slippery folds with his fingers.

Dark need claimed her senses, and she floated in a haze. The sting on her ass, the burn so deep inside. And Ty's rich, masculine scents. She couldn't get enough.

"You came down here for this, didn't you? Admit you were looking for me." He thrust two fingers into her pussy, high and tight. She quaked, almost lifted onto his fingers. Her muscles strained as her walls clenched madly around his invasion.

When she didn't answer, he withdrew his fingers. Punishing her in another way.

"Say you were looking for me."

"I..." She cast about for something snarky to say but words were beyond her. She needed him — his touch, his mouth.

"Bree." His voice was a warning.

Twisting her face on the pillow, she tried to see him. "Yes," she gasped.

"Good girl." He slid his fingers back into her pussy, making her pulsate. Somehow the absence of his touch almost thrilled her more than the actual caress. In the time between, her desire had built.

Rocking against his hand, she lost herself. He finger fucked her hard and she issued a long, guttural moan.

"That's it. Lose control with me because I'll take care of you. I'll give you whatever you want as long as you behave."

Breathless, on the verge of a release bigger than anything she'd ever known, she tried to wrap her head around his words. The threads slipped through her hands and she could only feel.

"Ty..."

"You want to come on my fingers, don't you? Soak them so I can lick them off." He plunged them faster, drawing her up onto her knees with each delicious motion. A fire swept through her. Pressure mounted.

The tip of one finger snaked out and grazed her clit.

With a scream, she came. Bursting, somersaulting, towed under the force of her release.

* * * * *

Ty couldn't get the condom on fast enough. He fumbled it into place, chest rising and falling as if he'd outrun a mad bull. He squeezed a copious amount of lube onto his fingers and spread it over Bree's ass.

She'd come to the ranch wanting this, and whether she admitted it or not, she wanted *him*.

As he readied her pucker with a lubed finger, she made tiny squeaks that drove him wild.

"I'm going to show you how good it can be, having me deep in your ass. Every minute afterward, you're going to remember who had you here." He eased a finger past the tight rim. The added lube aided his entry, and heat enveloped his finger.

For a moment, he couldn't breathe or think about anything but having that scorching warmth around his cock. He'd always loved ass play with a woman—or man—but something about having Bree was giving him a giddiness he didn't understand.

He added a second finger to her backside, stretching her slowly. When she loosened and started to push back, he scissored his fingers. Her small noises stole his mind. Biting off a curse, he removed his fingers and poised at her entrance.

"I'm going to love having your hot ass gripping me. If you try to sass me, I'll stop. Neither of us wants that."

"No." Her voice was a reedy wisp of its normal strength.

He leaned over her and kissed her. She gave herself to him fully, twisting to get at him. When he pulled free, he tangled the fingers of his other hand in her hair.

And stopped. Beneath the length of blonde strands, he felt a rougher patch. Almost as if it had been shaved.

She pushed upward, and he forgot about his discovery for a moment. He thumbed her globes apart, watching his swollen cap disappear into her tight heat.

Her breathing grew choppy.

"Relax. I've got you. I'll keep you safe."

She calmed, allowing him in an inch at a time. He gulped back a yell and watched her face, turned sharply on his pillow. After this, he'd never fall into his bunk without thinking of her. Her reaction dizzied him.

He sank in another inch. A bead of perspiration ran down her neck and disappeared around her collarbone. He wanted to lick it off.

After.

He had to have her — now.

With a purposeful shove, he sank into her body. She cried out, almost rolling up to meet him. He threw his head back and fought the need to thrust hard and deep. She was ripping down his wall of control, brick by brick.

"Ty," she almost pleaded.

"Yeah, baby girl?"

"Move."

He didn't even care that she hadn't asked but had commanded. He was helpless against her. With slow, gliding movements he took her. "Hell, you're so tight."

"I can feel every inch of you."

Her awed tone scrabbled at his senses. He withdrew almost to the tip before plunging back inside. "Who's fucking your ass?"

"You, Ty." A shuddering groan left her.

"Are you gonna come with me in your ass?"

She issued a staccato of gasps. "I…I want to. It's so good."

"But you need more?" He leaned over her, licking the shell of her ear while curling a finger around her nubbin. Her clit strained and when he flicked it, she bucked. Taking him to the balls, gripping his length.

"God yes. Baby girl, I have to come in your ass."

"Ty," she whimpered.

"Do you want to come?"

"Yesss."

He swirled his finger around her clit even as he ground into her ass. For her first time, she was taking him so…damn…well.

"Come for me, Bree."

As if she'd been waiting for his word, she jerked and twitched around him. He clung to her small noises while each spurt of his cock stole his sanity. Her cream drenched his fingers.

"When you're done coming…" he churned his hips, blind to everything but her noises, "…I'm going to throw your legs around my ears and lick you clean."

She pulsated around him, milking every last drop from his body. He slowed his movements and she collapsed, breathing heavily. He withdrew and as promised, guided her onto her back. Quickly he removed the condom. Then with each leg slung over his shoulders, he buried his tongue between her legs.

Her moan was ongoing, rising and falling as he lapped her up, moving lightly around her sensitive nub. When he snaked his tongue into her sheath, she contracted.

"Mmm. Look at me, Bree."

She did, eyes glassy. As he delivered the final slow licks to her folds, she grew boneless. When he moved up her body, placing soft kisses over her belly, breasts and finally claiming her mouth, she wrapped herself around him.

His heart flexed. Gathering her close, he buried his nose in her hair and drank in deep breaths of her soapy scent. For the moment she was tamed, and he loved her this way, all sweet and soft in his arms.

His heart resumed its normal rhythm.

Against his chest, she said, "Did I kill you?"

He grunted a laugh. "What makes you think that?"

"Your heart is so slow I wondered if it might have given out."

"I'm far from nearing the end." He trailed a hand up and down her spine.

"I'm good at mouth-to-mouth."

His smile reached all the way into his chest. "Is that so?"

"Yes. Though I once had a guy tell me I'm a bad kisser."

She was far from that. He'd given his share of kissing lessons, but Bree didn't need them.

"What did he say?"

"That my lips were too big."

"Are you kidding me?" They were perfect pink rosebuds he hadn't explored enough yet.

"No."

"What did you say?"

"I didn't say anything. I bit him."

He burst out laughing, envisioning it perfectly.

She giggled. "He yelled and asked why I did that. I told him I was showing him I have big teeth too."

Ty pinched her delicate chin and turned her face up. His gaze skimmed her full lips and the small but probably sharp teeth behind them. "They look good to me," he drawled.

"That's orthodontics. Daddy spent a fortune."

"How much of a fortune?" He wanted to keep her talking, amused by her stories.

She grinned, revealing straight white teeth. "As much as a good horse at auction."

"Sheesh. I'd rather have the horse." He slapped her ass, and she jerked against him. They struggled for a minute until she leaned in and lightly bit his lower lip, reminding him of the sore spot she'd left him with the other night.

How had they ended up in his bunk? Hell, she shouldn't be here at all. Yet he couldn't turn her away now. He caressed the curve of her ass, staring into her eyes. "Are you okay after what we did?"

She understood his meaning, goose bumps breaking out on her arms. "Yes."

"Good. Now cuddle up to me while I recover. Because we have a lot of hours between now and dawn."

She hooked her leg around his middle, her pussy damp against his skin. "Are you up for an all-nighter? Because I don't think you've got the stamina."

"Baby girl, I'm going to make you pay for saying that."

He thought that was exactly why she had.

Chapter Eight

Bree couldn't get the saddle on Royal fast enough. The horse danced in place, as eager as her rider. "I've almost got it," she said to the horse, then leaned forward and planted a kiss on its side.

She'd been lax in her nightly trick-riding practice, and while she had no intention of competing again, she missed it.

"There." She tightened the last strap and grabbed the pommel. Royal knew just what to do. She took off in a slow trot, and Bree ran alongside—one of the first tricks she'd learned—for ten steps, twenty, before vaulting into the saddle.

From the nearby paddock where a ranch hand worked with other horses, a cheer rose. Bree stood in the saddle and waved just as she would in the arena. He waved back, teeth white in his very tan face.

Royal got up to speed, and Bree relished the breeze. Since she'd left Ty's bed, she'd felt too hot. Not to mention too aware of the small pleasant aches from his lovemaking. His marks on her.

She had beard burn between her breasts after he'd worshipped them for half an hour. Her thigh muscle was strained from him placing it on his shoulder while sinking into her with maddening slowness. Not to mention the feel of him in her backside.

For a moment Bree lost her focus and let Royal gallop around the field.

What's wrong with me? It's just sex.

Then why was every other thought about Ty?

She'd replayed several moments on loop in her head, and strangely none of those involved the throes of ecstasy. She kept thinking about the in-betweens—his stories about his brothers or college.

Their discussion about ranching had really stimulated her, strangely enough. They'd compared notes on stock and the inner workings of a ranch. She'd finally trailed off, staring at the ceiling of the bunkhouse.

"What are you thinking?" Ty had leaned over her.

"I'm surprised at myself. I've never been too involved in the ranching. Daddy handles everything. I'm just a..." What was she? She belonged there, yes, but she didn't have anything she did well. She sort of drifted, finding busy work to occupy her time.

"Just a gorgeous woman with a lot of talent in bed?" Ty's drawl lured her from her thoughts.

She flashed him a grin. "Am I those things?"

"You're fishin' for compliments now, baby girl. Roll over so I can experience that talent." Once he had her where he wanted her, he placed his mouth to her ear. "You're a lot of things, Bree."

"Like what?" She shivered.

"Smart-mouthed."

She giggled, flexing her wrist in the grip of his fingers as he pinned her to the mattress.

"Funny."

Her giggle relaxed into a big smile.

"Sweet." He nuzzled her neck, and gooseflesh coated her every inch. "Daring. Too damn intelligent to get hooked up with some stupid ranch hand."

She stilled. "Why would I do that? I don't want to settle down with anybody."

He nipped her ear. "Good." He'd blown her mind after that, taking her to brand-new heights. But it was the conversation foreplay that stuck in her mind.

Did he really believe she was all those things?

She maneuvered herself in the saddle and did a forward bender, hanging off Royal, one knee bent. They looped. She thought some more.

When she flipped into the saddle again, she felt even less calm than she had before setting out to ride. Ty had knocked her off-balance. In giving her amazing pleasure he'd dug deep into her psyche.

She hung over the side of Royal again in a suicide drag, her hair and knuckles skimming the ground dangerously close to her horse's hooves. She'd once seen a rider do this trick and have a huge chunk of her hair ripped out. She'd come off her horse bleeding and clutching her head.

Bree had run her to the medics and seen her into the ambulance. The girl had lost some scalp and needed a skin graft. As far as Bree knew, she had a normal patch of hair growing there now.

Hoisting herself upright, she skimmed her fingers under her hair, over the velvety spot she kept shaved. Not in honor of that old friend but her mother.

Tears smarted in her eyes, but she stared at the horizon and willed them away. She'd done enough grieving. Sure, she missed her mom but she rarely dwelled on her loss. Everyone had a sob story, after all.

She whipped through several more tricks until her muscles were warm and tingly from exertion. When she stood in the saddle for her final gallop, the ranch hands cheered. Usually she ignored them, but this evening she waved and smiled.

Heart full, she returned Royal to her stall and brushed her.

Her father poked his head around the stall. "You get those chickens fed yet, Bree?" His brows were drawn together, punctuating his displeasure. Irritation engulfed her.

Shooing him away, she went back to brushing.

He blocked the entrance, hands on hips, taking up the whole space. "Bree, if you aren't pulling your weight on the ranch, you're going to have to return to waitressing."

God, she hated waitressing. Schlepping around with trays of food people complained wasn't right, and when she got mouthy in return she got nothing for a tip but a reprimand from her boss.

With a sigh she looked at her father. "I'm not waiting tables when I have a father who owns a ranch."

Immediately, she checked herself, almost looking around for Ty, expecting him to jump out and punish her for sassing. Sassing her father, no less. She met Daddy's gaze.

Swallowing hard, she said, "I'll go right now."

As she fed the chickens and gathered eggs, she couldn't help but wonder what Ty would have done to her if he'd witnessed the exchange with her father. A bead of perspiration rolled down her neck and into her collar.

Smart-mouthed. When she sassed Ty, his eyes blazed. While he wore that look, she'd come to expect mind-spinning torment followed by dizzying delights. In a short time together, they'd fallen into a rhythm that excited her beyond belief.

But her father only got mad. Why *didn't* she just do her chores in a timely manner? She wasn't lazy. She just didn't like being told what to do.

Unless Ty's giving the orders.

Inside she washed and changed in time to sit down at the long table with all the ranch hands and her father. Cook struggled into the room, balancing a heavy tray with each hand.

"Let me help you." Bree jumped up and took one of the trays. Cook smiled at her, face creasing in wrinkles. Bree moved around the table, dispensing baked beans and baskets of rolls.

As she neared the head of the table, her father cocked a brow at her. Not in question but in confusion.

Bree dropped him a wink and spun off to her seat. Once she plopped down between two burly men, she chanced a look at her father. He was still staring at her, a strange expression on his face.

She reached into the nearest basket and gripped a roll. "Think fast!" She tossed it right at her father's chest.

His big hand snagged it from the air, and they shared a smile. The strain between them vanished.

After dinner, Bree sprawled on her bed with her phone. She hadn't yet texted Ty, but he'd added his contact to her phone for a reason, right?

Heart thumping, she shot him a simple *hi*.

He responded instantly. *Hey, baby girl.*

Liquid heat pooled low in her belly. Too easily she heard his deep voice rumbling those words that lit her on fire every time.

I'm going to sneak onto the ranch tonight. She held her breath, bursting with mirth at the idea she was now telling him her intentions rather than just rolling under the fence and popping up someplace she didn't belong.

No.

Yes.

Bree, I have something to do tonight. I can't see you.

Her stomach plummeted to her bare toes. She gazed at the screen, twisting her lips. She didn't like thinking of Ty doing his job. In the beginning, knowledge of the Boot Knockers' duties sent a thrill through her. But after two nights in Ty's arms, the idea of him with another woman was a green ribbon of unease that tied her up in knots.

She pushed out a breath, thumbs poised over the keys. *There are plenty of other guys on the ranch.*

Like hell. No. Stay put.

Damn, she even liked him ordering her around via text. While part of her wanted to tempt him into saying he'd spank her for misbehaving, a deeper part wanted to please him.

Besides, he wouldn't just tell her to stay away if he really could spend time with her. She pictured him in bed with another woman and made a face.

I'm coming.

If I find you on this ranch, you're not going to like what happens.

No?

Try me and see. And don't you dare get off until you're with me.

She flopped onto her back, holding her phone above her face, burning. Maybe she should just call him.

I'll text you later.

Damn, was he brushing her off?

At the risk of sounding like a prying girlfriend, she thumbed, *What's going on?*

Fight. Gotta go.

For several long minutes she waited for more, but nothing came. A fight? Was Ty in the middle of it? She recalled him and the other Boot Knocker rolling in the mud, hard bodies slicked as they tried to hurt each other — because of her. Then Ty and the Dom in the auditorium…

If that was happening again, she needed to be there.

She sat up and swung her legs off the bed. But before she sank her toes into her plush carpet, she thought better of it. If Ty found her on the ranch, he really might be displeased enough to block her out. Not only keep her off the ranch but out of his bed.

Easing back to the bed, she ran her hands up and down her torso, then over her breasts that Ty didn't find lacking at all. Her nipples pebbled at the light touch, but she wasn't thinking of Ty's hands on her skin.

She was replaying the conversation about the good he saw in her, one more time.

* * * * *

Bree crowded closer to Ty, enveloped by his warmth. The wool blanket beneath them prickled her bare arms. "Is this a horse blanket? It's scratchy."

"Yeah, but a clean one. A cowgirl like you oughta be used to rough things." His voice was amused.

She skimmed a finger down his shirt buttons, all the way to his belt buckle. His abs seemed to ripple beneath her touch. "I like it rough." Did her blush sound in her voice? Crap, it did.

Ty squeezed her waist. Then in one swift move, he rolled her atop him, settling her against his every hard inch. She throbbed from his nearness — and her deprivation. She hadn't gotten off in two days, just as he'd commanded. A thrill went through her.

As she looked down into his face, her breath caught. Had she once thought he looked too boyish for her? His rugged, chiseled features were anything but boyish. And he hadn't shaved, which lent him the dangerous air she needed.

She brushed her fingers over his jaw. The rasping noise seemed to reach deep inside her and pluck chords she'd never heard before. "I love your five o'clock shadow."

"I know." His hard mouth quirked up at the corner.

She fought a shiver. "How do you know?"

"Because of your response when I rub it over you." His slowly drawled words lit her fires.

She pressed her aching breasts against his hard chest. "Why haven't you touched me tonight?"

"Looking at the stars isn't enough?"

She wriggled. "Maybe for someone who's had release in the past two days." It upset her to think of what Ty had done without her this week. She burrowed her nose against his cotton shirt and inhaled his spicy scent. Really, when had she become such a drippy female? She'd always prided herself on boldness and fearlessness. Her resistance to attachment had been part of the package, and she wasn't losing who she was because her stupid brain told her to be jealous.

He looked past her at the heavens above. The night sky swirled with stars and clouds and shadows on the moon. Yeah, it was beautiful, but more interesting than she was?

She jerked her knee, jabbing Ty's inner thigh.

He growled. "Don't try that again."

Lowering her head, she sank her teeth into the center of his pec, right over his nipple. He didn't flick an eyelash.

Pissed, she rolled back onto the itchy horse blanket, glaring at the sky.

A shadow covered her as he leaned over, but two could play his game. She didn't look at him.

"Pouting won't get you what you want."

"Neither does being nice."

"Aww. Were you being nice, baby girl?"

Her gaze flashed to his, and she set her jaw.

"I know this hot, little body needs release. I see your nipples poking your shirt and smell your arousal from under this miniskirt."

His voice sent scorching spikes of need through her. She breathed shallowly, turned on beyond belief by his words.

He continued, holding her gaze, evoking memories of his length buried deep in her core. She fisted the blanket.

"You need me."

She couldn't speak.

"Say it."

Whatever mind game he played teased her into a frenzy. "Yesss."

He didn't lay a finger on her, yet she felt the lick of his gaze and remembered his tongue in other places. "You're throbbing for me right now, aren't you?"

She whimpered; the burn tripled between her thighs.

"Remember whom you're throbbing for. Whom you've thought about for two days."

Irritation washed over her, and she found her voice. "Why do you want me to only think of you? There are plenty of Boot Knockers who want me."

If he was angered, he didn't show it. His eyes remained calm, binding her up inside. "That's true. Anyone would want you, but you'll only be thinking of me and what I do for you."

She grunted. "Anyone can make me come."

"Yes, but can they make you quiver like I am right this second?"

It was true—she quaked with need and excitement. His very voice aroused her.

"What if I tell you that J want you to fuck another man?"

Shock ripped through her. She pushed back onto her elbows then into a sitting position. He remained where he was, lounging on one side, a smile playing around his lips. "What are you talking about?"

"If I tell you whom to fuck..." his voice pitched low, tantalizing more, "...you'll obey me, won't you?"

She gaped at him. "What kind of kinky bastard are you?"

He rumbled a laugh. "I *am* kinky, and that's why you like me."

Of course he was right, but she wouldn't admit it. "I don't belong to you. I won't do everything you say just because you think you have some supreme rule over me."

He cocked a brow. "Don't I?"

Warmth spread through her belly and reached into her chest. She refused to answer.

With a finger tracing circles on her knee then up to her bare inner thigh, he said, "If I tell you I've arranged for you to sleep with Elliot, will you tell me no?"

Conflicting emotions slammed her system. She didn't know how to process his words. Yes, she wanted more experiences that pushed her buttons. And weeks ago, she'd thrown herself at Elliot. But now that Ty had arranged for the meeting to happen, she wasn't so sure.

She knotted her fingers together.

"I can see I've got you all tied up."

She raised her jaw. "Do not."

He curled himself inward, bringing his lips close to her knee. "I know you, Bree."

She swallowed hard and tried to come up with a smart retort, but her words were trapped beneath swirling emotions. Had anyone ever said that to her before? Hell no. More than that, no one had ever *wanted* to know her.

"How can you say you know me when all we've done is sleep together?"

"Because I'm good at reading people. Don't tell me that you don't respond to me in every way, because you do." He brushed his lips over her knee, sending spears of lust straight to her pussy. She sank her fingers into his thick hair, hoping he'd keep kissing all the way up to her soaking center.

"You wanted Elliot."

"Yes."

"He wants you."

Damn, that was hot. Maybe she'd listen to Ty after all.

"And I want you to have him."

She stopped breathing, drowning in this strange and thrilling gift. Taboo, giving her a new sex partner, and yet so damn mind-bending. She needed this, whatever Ty's game was. He knew how to play her perfectly.

His eyes were dark gems holding hers prisoner. "I want to see the bliss on your face as he makes you come. And to see you giving your all to him."

"Y-you'll be there?" Her voice quavered as dark desire wove through her.

"Of course, baby girl. You don't go where I don't."

She tightened her grip in his hair. For a heartbeat, she couldn't breathe or think. He turned her inside out. "When?" she finally rasped.

"He's waitin' for us down on the ranch. One of the clients left early and we've got a bungalow."

Her eyelids fluttered shut. All she wanted was a bungalow and a Boot Knocker of her own. Now she was getting a two-for-one deal without shelling out the mountain of cash.

"There's one condition." Ty's words made her open her eyes.

Figures. Now he'll get bossy. Her folds grew wetter. "What's that?"

"You only listen to me. And if you don't behave, you'll leave. Simple as that." He hooked a finger under her chin and drew her down as he pushed upward until his lips hovered near hers. "Are we in agreement?"

Her whole adult life she'd dreamed of having an encounter like that. As she stared into his eyes she felt bound to Ty. She was utterly vulnerable around him. He liked keeping her that way—and, holy hell, how she loved it.

"I'm in."

Chapter Nine

Ty finished knotting Bree's wrists to the bedframe and stood back to look at his handiwork. She was spread facedown, arms and legs splayed.

"Your safe word's longhorn?"

She nodded.

Elliot stared at Bree's taut body. Judging by the state of his erection, her juicy pussy beckoned to him too. That was good—Ty's plan was going to work.

Ty was going to show Elliot that they could have some hot, dirty fun together without emotional hang-ups. Sharing Bree was going to make things right between them while blowing her mind.

"Feeling okay, baby girl?"

"Yes," she moaned, well on her way to being that sweet, soft woman he adored. She looked at him, eyes wide, pleading.

He couldn't resist leaning over and kissing her long and deep. As he swirled his tongue through her mouth, he lost himself nearly as much as she did. But not totally. When he pulled away, she tried to follow him.

"I wasn't done kissing," she mouthed off.

"No?" He stared at her until she squirmed.

"No. You'd better live up to this and blow my mind, Ty."

He circled the bed, his erection jutting before him.

Elliot's gaze raked over him, his hunger barely checked. When Ty had asked him to be a third with Bree, he'd made it clear to Elliot that they were just fuck buddies having a good time with a woman. Elliot had nodded understanding and jumped at the chance.

Bree twisted her head to the side to try to see him. "What are you going to do to me?"

"Don't worry, baby girl. You'll get what you deserve."

"It'd better be several orgasms. How dare you order me not to come for two days? I'm dying here." As if to make her point, she yanked against the bonds, making the bed rattle.

"You're the one who obeyed. And what a good girl you are too." He switched on a brand-new vibrator. The slim wand hummed to life, and Bree's back arched in response. Ty shot Elliot a grin as he aimed the toy between her spread thighs. When he slid it over her soaking folds, she cried out. Pushing back, she tried to take the vibrator deep.

Ty coated it in her juices before fitting it alongside her clit. Not exactly where she wanted it, but enough to torment her. If she lay there long enough, she'd get off. But he wasn't going to let that happen.

She thrashed, blonde hair brushing her naked shoulders.

"She's gorgeous," Elliot breathed.

"Yes, she is."

Bree fell still, obviously liking them talking about her. She wanted men to desire her, and Ty would play to that need. But he'd also dig into her psyche and flip the switch that made her the sweet Bree who'd become his addiction.

"She's dripping wet."

"Well, I'm hard as stone." Ty turned to his fuck buddy, and Elliot sank to his knees before his straining cock. They stood behind Bree, and when Elliot's mouth pulled groans from Ty, she tried to see.

"M-move in front of me."

"You wanna watch a man suck my cock, baby girl?"

"Yes." Breathless and pink-faced, she squirmed against the toy that wouldn't give her what she really needed.

Elliot released him and moved closer to Bree, giving her the show of a lifetime. She watched with hooded eyes as Elliot drew Ty's cock right to the root, cupping his balls in one big hand. Sucking and kneading until Ty felt that tingle drawn up from deep in his spine.

He had the control of five regular men, but not tonight. He had to get off — fast. Then he'd have the stamina to fuck Bree properly later. Besides, Elliot's tongue was driving him mad, riding along the underside of his dick just the way Ty liked.

Holding Bree's glassy stare, Ty cradled Elliot's face and fucked his mouth. "God, you're so good at that."

Elliot rumbled, taking him a millimeter deeper. Bree's eyes clouded, and he thought she might be on the verge too. He hoped she got off at seeing his pleasure. Nothing could be hotter at this moment.

With short grunts, Ty rocked his hips. Elliot took him — all of him. And Ty burst in a blinding release. Elliot gulped him down, and

Bree mewled in frustration. Ty's mind buzzed as he emptied into his partner's mouth.

Ty stroked his knuckles over Elliot's rough jaw. "I needed your mouth wrapped around me."

Bree made a noise, and Ty looked at her. Her hair hung into one eye, and she looked mad. He smiled and pulled free of Elliot's mouth. Moving close to the woman strapped to the bed, he smoothed the hair from her face. Then he bent and kissed her briefly.

"More."

He stiffened. "You'd better start asking nicely for what you want."

She met his gaze, softening already because she loved this play as much as he did. With each of her demands he gained more control, until she finally gave in. She knew damn well what she was doing, and he adored every minute of it.

"Can I please have a kiss?"

He reached back and delivered a love tap to her ass that echoed through the room. She moaned, and Ty motioned for Elliot. "Kiss Elliot while I take care of punishing you."

Elliot knelt beside the bed and kissed her, probably tasting like Ty. The thought brought Ty to full arousal again.

Heart thundering, he knelt between Bree's spread legs. Her round ass wasn't nearly red enough. He gripped each cheek hard, making her cry out as Elliot tongue-kissed her. They looked so good together, but in the back of Ty's mind he recognized that if he'd walked in to find them kissing, he'd have gone off like a cannon. Only because he'd ordered this did it turn him on.

He bit back a laugh. In the years since becoming a Boot Knocker, he'd turned into one sick fuck.

He slapped Bree's ass, lifting the tender skin with ten swift smacks. She squealed and fought. The bed shook with her struggle. Then he turned to her other cheek, and she stilled.

The next ten blows she rocked up to meet his hand.

Elliot raised his head and shared a smile with Ty.

"She wants a cock in her mouth. Don't you, Bree?" Ty asked.

"Uhhh."

Ty pushed on the vibrator, pressing it against her clit hard enough to bring her to the peak. "If you want to come, you need to help Elliot first since he was so good to me. Do you think you can take him? All of him?"

She nodded.

In his time on the ranch, Ty had done some crazy shit, but this would stick out in his memory forever. He was fueled by primitive lust and guided by an instinctual knowledge of how to take care of Bree.

She swallowed Elliot's cock, and Ty thrust the vibrator into her pussy. Elliot groaned, tangling his fingers in her silky hair and drawing her closer, closer.

"You only get him because I want you to have him. Is that clear, baby girl?" Ty angled the vibrator upward, scraping the inner spot of her pussy that made her arch off the bed.

"Mmm-ahh." She closed her eyes and sucked, cheeks hollowing. As Ty watched, he lost himself to the rhythms of her body. When her pussy gripped the vibrator, Ty pulled it out and settled it over her straining nubbin once more.

Her body jerked and the bed creaked as she came. Bliss captured her beautiful features, causing Ty's chest to tighten. Juices squeezed from her folds, and Ty gathered some on his finger, painting it over her thickened lips.

"Don't let her get you off," he said to Elliot. Their gazes locked. "That's my job."

Bree issued a ragged groan, her whole body twitching. Elliot moved away, cock still stretching toward Bree's gorgeous full lips.

God, Ty could play like this all night. And from Bree's responses, he bet she could too.

He teased her pussy with his wet finger, opening her. "You're going to take Elliot here while I fuck him. Yes?"

She nodded frantically, still riding her afterglow.

Elliot got a condom and slid it over his stiff cock as Ty stretched Bree with one finger then two. Finally he inserted the vibrator and fucked her nice and slow, readying her for Elliot.

"He's thick. Can you take him?"

"Mm-hmm."

"Good." He left the toy vibrating in her and kissed the length of her golden spine. Her skin tasted of soap and sweet woman, befuddling him with protectiveness. As he kissed over her spine and up to one shoulder, he felt her filling a hollow space in his chest he hadn't realized was there. Like digging a hole and having clear, fresh springwater rush into it.

Closing his eyes, he dropped soft pecks to her arm and around to nuzzle her ear. She turned into his kiss, wild with need. He took her mouth for long minutes, almost forgetting Elliot was in the room until he made a low noise.

Ty lifted his head and riveted him with his stare. "You're nice and lubed?"

"Yes." Elliot breathed heavily.

Passion flared, and in seconds he sheathed his own cock in a condom. He added ample lube to the head and slowly circled the bed. He and Elliot came together in a clash of mouths. Their tongues invaded, and they rubbed against each other cock to cock. Bree strained. Damn, the little vixen was getting off on this more than he'd ever thought. It was a heady sensation — one he couldn't get enough of.

So much for getting her out of his system.

He broke away and gripped Elliot's biceps. Maneuvering Elliot until he knelt between Bree's legs, he watched Bree fall still. Elliot switched off the vibrator and tossed it aside.

"Take him, baby. Then I'm going to sink into him and drive him into you until you can't stop coming."

A guttural moan left her. Slowly, Elliot filled her.

"God, she's tight."

She cried out.

Ty caressed the hard planes of Elliot's ass, chest burning with wild need to plunge deep. Whatever was happening with him and Bree, Ty would never give up having other men. If he and Bree became a couple, he imagined them sharing a man on a regular basis.

What the hell am I thinking?

He stopped thinking altogether as he poised his swollen cock at Elliot's entrance. His partner withdrew from Bree, and when he sank to the balls again, Ty entered him. Elliot's breath whooshed out, and they all fell still.

"Please? Ty." Bree's whisper triggered something in Ty.

He needed her screaming while he was pounding into Elliot.

With a jerk of his hips, he took over. They fell into a smooth pace — push, pull, hard, fast, slow and deep. Ty bit into Elliot's shoulder, mind barreling along a slippery road to heaven.

Bree's noises grew louder, out of control. She tugged against her ropes. Elliot's body smacked hers and Ty's chest glued to his friend's back.

"Ty?"

Her plea broke through his sexual haze. "Baby?"

"Can I...come?"

Her words flipped a switch in him. With a roar, he reached around Elliot and clamped a hand on Bree's hip. "Come all over him. Now, Bree."

Breath rasping in her lungs, she stiffened. Twitched. And came.

* * * * *

Elliot's length jerked hard inside Bree as she tumbled through the warm, dark waters of release. His lips latched on to her neck, sucking. And all she could think of was Ty giving her this mind-blowing moment.

Her entire body felt as if she'd been electrified. The day she'd rolled under the fence, determined to find what she wanted on the Boot Knockers Ranch, was the best of her life.

As her breathing resumed a normal rate, she drifted. Could any of the other Boot Knockers have given her this kind of pleasure? Or could Elliot have done so without Ty driving him?

Everything in her life before this seemed small. For years she'd been trying to get her life in order and suddenly it felt possible. First, she planned to sit down and have a heart-to-heart with her father about her ranch duties. She needed something bigger than feeding chickens.

Up to this point, she hadn't shown she was responsible enough to handle anything else. But after talking with Ty about ranching, she realized she needed to be on the other end of it. Maybe in Daddy's office with his books, managing sales of livestock and instructing the ranch foreman.

Ty moved first, jarring her from her thoughts. When Elliot left her body, she released a long moan. Seconds later, hands worked over the ropes holding her ankles and wrists. She ached deliciously from the things they'd done to her. Her belly burned with anticipation. They had a long night ahead. More to come.

Ty took her in his arms and kissed her. Sweetness rose inside of her, and she poured it into the kiss. Clinging to him as their tongues mated.

When he let her go, he rubbed her wrists, which were reddened by the ropes. "You okay?"

"Yes." *Totally, mind-blown okay.*

He caught Elliot's hand and drew him down on the bed with them. She watched the cowboys together, awed by the strength and power between them. It was obvious Ty was fond of Elliot, but the big, dark-haired man looked as if someone had lit a fire in him.

He wanted more from Ty.

As Ty wrapped her close and Elliot molded his body to Ty's back, Bree wondered at who Ty really was. She didn't know nearly enough. Would he ever fall in love with a man?

Ty was staring at her lips. She ran her tongue over them, feeling her power but not willing to wield it. Not when he felt so good and she was so peaceful.

He nestled his hand on her nape, fingers warm in her hair. His expression made her feel beautiful and cherished. When she glanced over his shoulder at Elliot, pain crossed the man's face.

Her heart constricted as she realized they were sharing a moment that didn't involve him.

As if understanding this too, Ty reached back and trailed his hand over Elliot's hard thigh. But she felt the change in the air.

* * * * *

When she awakened a while later, she was alone in bed. She tried to sit up and found the prickly fibers of a rope against her skin as Ty swished a length back and forth against her skin. The all too familiar buzz of the vibrator sent shocks of need through her nerves. She gave him a smile.

As Ty brought the tip of the toy against her clit, she flexed, burning to get closer. "Easy, baby. It's just you and me and we're going to take our time." A blindfold came around her eyes, cutting off the sense she needed.

"What do you mean we're alone?"

"Elliot had something to do."

"What? No, Ty. He can't leave."

"He did. You got your threesome."

"No, it's not about me. Ty, he's hurting. He felt left out—"

The bed sank beneath her, and she rolled against Ty's hard body. He sighed, making her wish she could see his face. "He has a client this week and had to get back to her."

There was more. What had she missed? Sex had worn her out and she wished she hadn't fallen asleep. "Oh…"

"I promise you won't miss not having two cocks. I can take care of you."

She twitched as he reached between her legs and angled the vibrator to spear her pussy. She flooded, groaning. But she wasn't ready for sex yet. She wanted—needed—to talk to him.

"Wait." Her hands were still free and she found his wrist. "Can't you just…"

He switched off the vibrator but didn't remove it from her pussy. "Yes, baby girl?" His voice caressed.

"Can we lie here and talk for a while?"

There was a smile in his voice. "With or without the blindfold?"

"Without. I'd like to see you."

A beat of silence passed. "Since you asked so nicely, I can't deny you. Can't deny you anything," he muttered.

As he removed the toy, untied her legs and got rid of the blindfold, a new desire sprang up. She reached out for him, and he came into her arms. When he rested his head between her breasts, arms tight around her, she swallowed hard.

"I shouldn't like this as much as I do." His admission raised a knot of emotion into her throat. He wasn't the only one.

What was wrong with her anyway? She'd just refused sex—blindfolded, no less—to cuddle? She needed to find a shrink ASAP.

She drew deep breaths of his scent. After a minute, she asked, "Are you sure Elliot's okay?"

"Yeah, he's all right. He knows I don't want anything more than what we have."

"What's that?"

"Sex. Fun. Good times and friendship."

"I think he wants more."

Ty nodded, hair soft against her breasts. "I probably made a mistake in asking him to join us. But he's the only one I'd trust with you. I thought this would make it clear we were just having fun and it wasn't anything more."

"It ended up hurting him."

"Yeah. I screwed up."

"It *was* amazing, though." Her mind was invaded with images from their encounter.

"Yes, it fucking was."

She brushed her lips over his head. "I loved every second."

"Good." He looked up at her, and her insides melted. After a long heartbeat, he asked, "You feel this, don't you?"

Suddenly she wanted to run. Thank God her ankles were unbound. "What?"

"You thought sex was all you wanted, but I showed you that what you needed was the connection."

His words slammed into her and her mind seemed to pause. Was he right? The link they'd shared had heightened the pleasure, but did she want a link with Ty? She didn't know. She needed time to think.

She tensed, preparing to bolt. But Ty began kissing her breasts, eyes closed, moving his lips over each with such tenderness that she couldn't bear to leave his arms.

When his mouth closed over a nipple, her walls crumbled. He was right about her needing a connection — so right.

Chapter Ten

Ty nudged Elliot's shoulder. The man looked up at Ty holding his tray of food. Without a word, he scooted down the bench to make room. Fighting a heavy sigh, Ty settled beside him but didn't dig into his breakfast burritos.

Elliot picked at his with a fork.

"We need to get this out in the open, man," Ty said. He'd messed up bad. His plan had backfired, especially when all his feelings for Bree had surfaced during the ménage.

Elliot stiffened but didn't look at him. "What's that?"

"What's going on between us." Ty glanced around, glad Elliot had sat by himself today.

"You made it pretty clear there's nothing going on between us." Elliot's tone was dead.

Ty finally released a sigh. "I want to make sure you're okay."

"Never better." Elliot picked up a burrito and took a bite so enormous it would render him speechless for a couple minutes.

Dammit, Ty had really screwed up. He'd known Elliot craved more with a man. Ty should have...what? Ignored him? They were friends first. In his mind, he'd defined boundaries but Elliot had read it all wrong.

Asking him into the bedroom as a third was a huge error in judgment that had hurt his friend and made Ty feel like shit.

"Look, man, we're friends."

Somehow Elliot managed to swallow his big bite. His eyes blazed. "Oh yeah. Friends who fuck."

"Exactly. It might sound strange to outsiders, but this is the Boot Knockers Ranch."

"What are you doing with Bree?"

Confusion trickled into his mind. "What?"

"You have women every night of the week. You left a client unattended to have a ménage with Bree. Are you gonna tell me you were doing some duty?"

Hell. "No."

"You want that woman for yourself. I saw you with her, Ty." Elliot poked a finger toward his chest.

Crap. How was he going to keep Elliot from being hurt further? He glanced around, ensuring no one was near enough to overhear—especially Hugh.

"You knew what you were getting into when you signed up. I said it was just sex."

Elliot's face mottled red. "I goddamn do remember. I remember every moment we've been together, Ty. The first time you took me outside after a poker game and kissed me. When we shared that first girl. Hell, I can't even remember her name now! But I remember what you did to me that night in vivid detail."

"You've been with Jeremy. I thought..."

"You thought wrong. He's not you."

"When I told you that we were only doing it for Bree, you said 'of course'. I took it that you really got that."

"I thought I did. Until I was with you again."

Dropping his head, Ty ached from the pain he'd caused his friend. Elliot had been attached to Jack. Now Ty had ripped Elliot open again.

He met Elliot's gaze. "You're one of my best friends," he said again as if it would leave an impression and ease the strained look on Elliot's face.

Elliot launched to his feet and practically jumped over the bench. "Save it. And next time you need a third, find someone else."

As Elliot stalked away and dumped his tray with a crash, Ty's chest burned. Several Boot Knockers looked at him, but he ignored them. Let them talk. It didn't matter. He wasn't in a relationship with Elliot, allowing his heart to get in the way of his job duties. He hadn't broken any rules. He'd made it plain to Elliot he wasn't interested in more.

Then why did it bother him so much?

"Fuck." Abandoning his burritos, he dumped his tray too and left the grub house. The day was bright and sunny, a good day for the final rodeo of the week. Too bad he felt far from entertaining. The idea of getting into his chaps and giving the ladies a show they'd remember held no appeal.

More and more he'd found himself going through the motions of his job rather than enjoying it.

He drank in a big gulp of the grass-scented air and started walking.

He didn't realize his intent until he arrived at his truck. He climbed in and groaned as Bree's sweet, soapy scent struck him. She'd been in the truck with him last. He'd driven her home and dropped her at the front door as boldly as if they'd been on a date.

Son of a bitch, why wasn't he able to unplug from her? He was failing miserably at keeping his distance.

He stuck his key in the ignition and twisted it. The short drive to the Roberts ranch wasn't long enough to allow him to put his mind in order. He was running on pure instinct again. As always with Bree.

The Robertses' cook admitted Ty to the house and led him to the office where Dan sat behind his desk, wire-framed glasses perched low on his nose as he pored over some papers.

He looked up, his expression hardening. "What's the little hellion done now?"

Ty almost laughed. So they were united in their opinions of Bree. "Nothing, as far as I know."

Dan sat back and removed his glasses. Gesturing to the chair opposite the desk, he said, "Have a seat. What brings you here if my daughter hasn't led you on some wild chase?"

Ty wasn't so certain she hadn't, but it wasn't in the sense Dan meant. Bree had tangled herself up in Ty's life. He was here...

Why *was* he here?

He stared at her father for a heartbeat, trying to make sense of his thoughts.

"You look confused, son. Is this to do with my daughter?"

He nodded slowly.

"Spit it out. I've got work to do, and so do you, more'n likely."

"I was wondering what makes Bree the way she is, sir."

Dan drew up straight, eyes eagle sharp. "What do you mean?"

"I mean...what makes her buck the rules?"

With a huff of a sigh, Dan sank against his chairback. "You wouldn't be asking if she weren't bucking."

"I just need to know."

"I can see why you came to me, but I can't explain it any more than she probably could. She was always a sassy little thing. At three, she wore some big boots on this ranch. Everyone coddled her. I'm just as guilty as my ranch hands and her mother."

"And you think this is why she got out of control?" The only times Ty had seen her in control was when he held the reins. Those moments he saw a peace and joy in her that broke his damn heart. She deserved that every minute of every day.

Dan picked up a photo frame and spun it for Ty to see.

A lump clotted his throat as he took the picture and looked more closely. A beautiful woman who looked a lot like Bree, but bald. Bree had mentioned her mother's battle with cancer, and this brought it home. Especially since Bree stood beside her mother, her head shaved in support.

He swallowed hard and met Dan's eyes, which were bright with unshed tears. "They were close, you can see. Took a long time after...after my wife died...for Bree's hair to grow in."

Not all of it. She kept one small part underneath shaved. In reminder? Must be. God, Ty wanted to wrap her in his arms and tell her that he knew and it was okay. He'd take care of her emotions that had gotten so out of whack. Suddenly he knew this with a bone-deep certainty.

He'd also bet the job he loved that he was the first and only one who could make Bree feel that peace and joy.

"I'm sorry for your loss, Mr. Roberts. I think I understand Bree a bit better."

He stared at Ty for a long minute. "Do I need to ask why you need to understand her better?"

Ty stood. "No. You probably understand it more than I do at this moment. Thank you for your time."

* * * * *

"Daddy, can I talk to you?" Bree poked her head around the office door.

He got to his feet. "Must be serious if you're not just barging in like the daughter I know."

Her face heated as she came into the room and closed the door behind her. She'd always loved this space. The wood and leather, the big desk. And photos of their family and various ranch hands who'd become like family over the years.

"Is this about that Boot Knocker?"

She jolted. "What Boot Knocker?"

"The one who came here today. Ty."

Oh God. Panic swept her. What had Ty come for? She racked her brain for something she'd done to displease him then checked herself. He'd invited her to the ranch for that ménage.

But Ty wouldn't have told her father about the threesome. What happened between them was private. The things she did with Ty weren't anything to be ashamed of and Ty would never put her on public display.

Not unless I asked for it.

Feeling the pitch and heave of her new thought patterns, she sank to the leather chair. "What was Ty doing here?"

"Just asking some questions." Her father waved a hand in a dismissive gesture. "What do you want to discuss?"

She wasn't finished asking about Ty yet, but for now she'd follow her daddy's lead. "It's about the ranch and my duties on it."

"If you think you're getting out of cleaning that coop—"

"No," she said a bit too loudly. Her father stopped. "I'll do the chickens without complaint from now on. But I'm here because I want to do more."

"More? As in…"

"Maybe you could teach me about the upcoming auction? How to select which horses go to sale and how many head of cattle to sell off?"

Shock registered on her father's face. It shouldn't be funny because he didn't believe her capable of asking such a question. She couldn't suppress her smile, though.

He sat back. "You're asking to get more involved on the ranch?"

"Yes."

"What's brought this on? You've never shown an interest before."

She shrugged. "I can't flit around forever. Besides, you spent good money to send me to college to be able to manage the ranch someday."

He propped his jaw on his fist and stared at her as if she'd grown a second head. Hell, the way she felt, she wouldn't be surprised to look in the mirror and see one had sprouted. Her night with Ty had left her shaken. Mostly because she didn't know who she was anymore. Requesting a cuddle instead of the amazing orgasms he could give her? Wanting to get into his mind and find out who he was?

She shook herself.

"You're right, Bree. It's time for you to learn what goes on behind this desk so you can manage what happens out there." He pointed to the window and the fields beyond.

"I'm ready."

"Then have a look at this." He pushed a sheet of paper toward her. She sucked in a breath when she spotted the Boot Knockers Ranch logo at the top. It was a paid invoice.

"A hundred head of longhorn?"

"That's right. Coupla guys bought them to start a herd of their own. Best stock around, they said." Pride infused her father's voice.

"So how can I help?"

"With organizing a cattle drive. Since our ranches are neighboring, there's no need to freight them by truck. You can organize a group of hands to herd them over the border and up to the property where they want them."

She nodded. How had she gotten into a position where she was moving cattle onto a property that a week ago she'd been banned from? It was so ridiculous she laughed.

Her father cocked a brow. "Are you up for it?"

"Of course." She shared a smile with her father, warmed by the admiration in his eyes.

"Now I need some answers." Immediately she revised her demand. "Please."

"About?"

"Ty. Why was he here?"

"Asking about you."

Excitement flitted through her system. "What about me?"

"He asked why you were such a rule breaker."

Oh no. "What did you say?"

Her father grinned. "Told him you'd always been this way."

What had Ty said about that? She could almost feel his hand on her ass, bringing her to a fever of arousal.

Her tripping heart screamed that she was falling for him. That couldn't happen. She wasn't finished sowing her oats. When visiting the ranch in the future, she'd have to be careful to avoid Ty. The fun she wanted; the ties, not so much.

Ty made her feel too...off-balance. He drew out her vulnerable side and exposed her in ways that left her feeling more naked than she'd been while mudding on that ATV. She didn't like being out of control.

When she glanced at her father, he was studying her. Thankfully, he didn't say a word about the questions he must have about Ty. He only gestured for her to come around the desk so they could make notes about how to start moving those cattle.

But her heart was still racing at an insane pace, and her mind tumbled. It was silly and childish to think she'd have a chance at stealing a Boot Knocker and making him into her very own. She didn't want to, anyway. That meant she needed to keep Ty at arm's length.

* * * * *

The women in the stands were going wild for Elliot, who was on a bucking bronc for the final rodeo of the week.

Ty stood on the sidelines with Riggs, watching the man who'd made a wide path around Ty when he spotted him. Ty didn't have to wait long before Riggs butted into his business.

"Whatever happened between you, he's taken it hard."

Pushing a breath through his nose, Ty nodded. "I gave it to him straight, that's all."

"You did the right thing. Cutting it off before he got too hurt to work here is best."

As Ty stared at his friend, his exchange with Elliot minutes before the rodeo rose in his mind, hot and barbed.

"I don't want to hurt you, man. I care for you."

"But not in the way I care for you." Elliot's movements were jerky as he pulled on his chaps.

"We've got this—" he swept a hand through the air to indicate the ranch, "—and that's enough. Right?"

"Don't you ever get sick of not having a connection for more than a friggin' week at a time?" Elliot's eyes were dark with pain.

"That's where friends come in. They fill a hole in my life, but we both know it can't go beyond bodily pleasures and friendship, Elliot."

"You say you don't want a relationship, but we're dropping like flies. The Boot

Knockers aren't as content as we once were—fuck 'em and leave 'em isn't so good anymore. Tell me—why are you playing with Bree when you don't have to?" He looped rope around his fist and eyed Ty.

Ty's heart did a slow dive. This was it then. From here on out, he and Elliot's friendship would be strained. Pained.

* * * * *

The crowd cheered, knocking Ty back to earth. Elliot was poetry on the back of that bronc, curling forward at the right times, using his arm to counterbalance himself. Watching him almost made Ty wish he had feelings for the man. But if it were meant to be, he would have fallen for him long ago. His feelings would be evident.

Like they were for Bree.

Shit. No. I don't need to love anybody. I need to do my job well and enjoy life. He'd never answered Elliot's question and it bugged him. He felt as if he needed to explain why he was playing with Bree, but the words were jumbled in his mind.

Riggs clapped him on the back, jarring him from his thoughts. "He'll come around in time. You'll have your friendship back."

"I hope." Ty wondered if Riggs had ever felt that way about Hugh—that in time he'd stop loving the man and resume their old camaraderie.

A few feet away Stowe stood with legs braced apart and whip in hand. The Dom went into the ring wearing a pair of assless chaps that always roused the ladies. Instead of taming women in chains and collars, he had a great routine with horses.

Ty nodded at Riggs and moved toward Stowe. They'd parted on very bad terms and he didn't like having strife in the workplace. All over Bree.

Damn, why did she rile him so much?

Stowe's gaze was steady. "Need something, Ty?"

"Yeah." Never one to mince words, he just said it. "I need to apologize. I shouldn't have thrown punches that day in the auditorium."

Stowe's mouth relaxed. "Me either. We don't need to fight over women when there are so many to be shared."

"True."

"Except you weren't sharing that day, Ty. What's that about?"

Crap. He didn't need Stowe filling Riggs's shoes, bringing him up on charges of liking someone too much. Especially Bree. She didn't belong here. Sleeping with Elliot was one thing — Bree was quite another.

"She's young. She wasn't ready."

"She's old enough and was quite ready. The young ones are easier to train. They slip into the life with little trouble."

Ty's shirt felt too tight. He shifted his shoulders. "She doesn't belong here."

"She was one of the first ones I've enjoyed since — " He broke off, staring at the far-off horizon. "Are you trying to protect her from us or us from her?"

Good question. "She's better off staying away from the ranch. Once women get into that headspace with you, they crave more."

"And you can't have her wanting to return to me. Especially since *you* want to be doing the taming. Is Bree the brat you told me about?"

Ty nodded.

Stowe shot him a grin. When Ty had no reply, Stowe gave a practice flick of his whip. "No worries, mate. We're square, you and I."

Ty man-hugged him and walked away. As he strode across the patch of turf leading to the bunkhouse, he couldn't think straight. What Stowe had said was like an asteroid headed straight to the earth. He had a life plan, good work. Bree had struck him, hollowed out a Bree-sized crater in his chest.

Son of a bitch. What was he going to do about evicting her from his life? He could ignore her and hope she didn't return to the ranch, but that wouldn't happen. Soon he'd find her in the arms of another Boot Knocker. Hell, she'd be under Stowe's whip in a heartbeat, knowing the way she needed dominance in a man. If Ty ever found her with another of his friends, he'd lose his shit even more than he had before.

He doffed his hat and raked his fingers through his hair. Thank goodness he'd done his clown bit early in the rodeo because he needed to get away. The ranch felt too close, too crowded. In the past, he'd go find someone—maybe even Elliot—and they'd have a quickie against the bunkhouse. But those days were over.

Bree had wormed her way between them too.

"Dammit." He yanked his hat back on and pulled the brim low. His truck keys were in his pocket and he had a wallet full of cash. He'd leave for the day. Drive into the next county where nobody knew him. Maybe drink beer and watch the game on a big screen without thinking about sex and mouthy little vixens who drove him crazy.

When he got in his truck, he didn't head out to the interstate, though. As he bumped up in front of the Roberts Ranch, irritation mingled with a touch of excitement. Bree was behind those doors. He'd bring her out and put her into his truck, listen to her sass while he drove her into the next county and plied her with a steak dinner and enough margaritas to soften her before he ever laid a hand on her round ass.

He got out of his truck and seconds later her father appeared. "What brings you up here?" Judging by his voice, he already suspected.

Ty tipped his hat out of respect. "Looking for your daughter, sir."

"She isn't here."

"No?"

"She went to stay with family in Omaha for a spell."

Of all the things Ty expected to hear, that wasn't it. Dan's words felt like a blow to the chest, leaving Ty leaking air. He ran a hand down his shirt buttons. "When do you expect her to return?"

"I don't rightly know. She wanted to learn about ranching, and I thought she'd have new experiences with her relatives. She's always been close with a cousin out there too."

"I see. That's good."

"Good for her but not for you, I suspect." Dan's eagle eyes glued Ty to the ground.

He waved a hand. "I...was just coming to ask her something. Nothing important. I'll catch up with her later."

He could text her. Or call. But having her out of reach while she mouthed off wouldn't do—he couldn't take control the way she wanted.

And *he* needed.

Hell, what a mess. She had him knotted up.

Ty thumbed his hat brim again. "Thank you for your time. I'd best get back to the ranch."

He didn't drive to the ranch, though. He headed down the gravel lane and out to the main road. The gray ribbon of asphalt took him as far as the next town before he stopped and warmed a barstool long into the night. And when he was unable to drive home, he slept in his truck.

And dreamed of Bree.

Chapter Eleven

Two weeks in Omaha and Bree still hadn't gotten over the fact her daddy had shipped her off there like a little kid or a head of cattle. He hadn't even *asked* her—just handed her a slip of paper with a flight number.

"What's this?" she'd asked.

"Your aunt and uncle have agreed to let you come see how they do things on their ranch for a couple weeks."

"I already know what goes on. I grew up on a ranch, remember?" Irritation webbed inside her brain, catching any sane thought she may have before it reached her lips.

"You came to me and said you want to work. Since then, you've put in maybe three days of work before going back to your old ways. You won't get away with being lax up in Omaha, Bree. It will do you some good. Especially if you're interested in really pulling your weight around here. Or have you changed your mind?"

She felt like stomping her foot then thought better of it. Ty would paddle her behind. She pressed her lips together and stifled a scream. "No, I haven't changed my mind." Her words came out like bullets. Heat infused her face and she tried not to crumple the paper in her fist.

Her father nodded and went back to his paperwork. "Good to hear. You'll enjoy your time with family, and they can teach you things."

She'd seethed all the way there, angry that her father had picked a damn poor time to decide she needed to learn the ropes of ranching with her aunt and uncle. She didn't want to be away from the Boot Knockers Ranch.

God, she was a mess. She wanted to be there—she didn't. Which was it? Maybe going to Omaha would help organize her thoughts. She'd believed putting some distance between her and Ty would help her immensely.

She'd been wrong.

And that was the last damn time her daddy treated her like a kid. She was an adult and could make her own damn decisions. Her first decision had been to come home from Omaha early. After being away, she felt more attuned to the things she needed to do to prove herself on the ranch. She intended to start today.

With a sigh she smoothed her hands over her shirt. It had taken her two tries to get it buttoned right while half-asleep. But she was here, gathered outside with the other ranch hands getting the day's orders as dawn lightened the sky. Usually she was awake at this time but lounged in bed until she felt like getting up. But for the past two weeks when she'd stayed with her family, she'd been awake before sunup. Her cousin was a year younger than Bree but she had her sights set on ranching and had teased her mercilessly about not getting out of bed.

Her family's spread outside of Omaha wasn't as big as the Robertses', but Bree got a chance to work alongside them and learn things. Yeah, she had a degree in agriculture and business but her hands-on experience had been lacking — because she hadn't bothered.

Daddy's right.

She listened to her father dole out duties. Three men were sent to do a daily check for injured or sick animals. Two to the ridge to fix some leaning fence.

Bree's chest squeezed as she thought about that ridge, and what lay beyond — the Boot Knockers Ranch.

Ty.

Running to Omaha hadn't helped her escape that man. He'd possessed her even from hundreds of miles away. She'd thought about texting him a hundred times, but he hadn't gotten in touch with her. Besides, it wasn't any fun to tease him when she couldn't relieve the ache of being away from him.

Had he thought about her at all? He'd probably been relieved not to have to drag her off their ranch.

She hooked her thumbs in her back pockets and waited for Daddy to give her a job. But he didn't. When the men dispersed and she still stood there, hurt and confusion hit her senses. She turned to her father. "What about me?"

His brows rose. "I'm glad to see you have your drive back."

"More so."

"Good. C'mon then. I've got a job for you."

Once she was seated in the office with a stack of auction papers before her, she felt slightly better. At least her father hadn't blown her off. She took up a calculator and began logging the cattle prices into the ledger.

But within minutes her mind wandered back to Ty. Her cousin had asked about her habit of daydreaming. When Bree had refused to say a word, her cousin had guessed it was a man Bree was thinking about.

She had to get Ty out of her system. That was a dead end with a capital *D*. He didn't want her; she didn't want him. They'd had fun and he'd given her some mind-blowing sex, but...

Not seeing him again made her heart spasm. She shoved the feeling away and worked till noon.

Her father came in and out of the office. Finally he clamped a hand on her shoulder. "You don't need to do a year's worth of work to make up for lost time, Bree. Break for lunch."

"Okay." She shoved the papers away and dug her thumbs into her eyes, rubbing.

She stopped and lowered her hands. She'd seen Ty rub his eyes that way. Had she picked up the habit?

"Oh. I almost forgot," her father said.

She pivoted to stare up at him. He looked better than he had since Mom had died — stronger. Thank goodness. Seeing him bearing that much grief had hurt Bree almost as bad as losing her mother.

"A man was here looking for you."

She stopped breathing.

"Wh-who?"

"A cowboy. A Boot Knocker."

Her heart did a wild tumble. "Why?" That couldn't be her voice. She'd never sounded that way in her life. "Oh, he must have been here about the cattle they bought?" Whoever *he* was.

"No. We drove those cattle across the border last week."

Damn, she'd missed it. She'd wanted to show up on the ranch and actually have a good reason to be there. Who was she kidding? She'd wanted to flaunt herself in front of Ty until he got that burning look in his eyes.

Daddy scratched his chin. "It was that fella Ty came looking for you."

She wanted to stand but her knees were weak. "When?"

"Day or two after you left. He hasn't been back. Not sure what he needed." Her father's gaze bore into her. He knew damn well what Ty wanted.

Bree found the strength to get to her feet. She felt the need to explain Ty to her father, but what could she say? *I sneaked onto the ranch and he did things to me no man has ever done. Or probably will again.*

Emptiness hollowed her stomach. Crap.

Wait — he came looking for me. Left the ranch and his job and came to find me.

Excitement made her feel giddy, like a little kid on Christmas Day. It took all her willpower not to bounce up and down.

Some hard truths sobered her. Until that minute she'd been lying to herself. She didn't want any old Boot Knocker. She wanted Ty to pursue her and to affect him as much as he affected her.

She left the office and ate lunch with her ranch family. Listening to their stories and watching their antics didn't make her feel any lighter. Neither did her father's solemn gaze.

As she toyed with one of her favorite dishes, chicken and biscuits, her mind tried to unknot the mystery of Ty's visit. He hadn't texted her or attempted to call her. Why would he? But he'd come to the ranch looking for her. That had to mean something.

Avoiding her father's stare, Bree got up and gathered her plate. "I'll be taking Royal out for the afternoon. Been too long since she's been exercised."

"Okay, daughter." He looked at her for another heartbeat before the foreman commanded his attention.

Bree slipped away to the kitchen and took care of her plate. Then she fluffed her hair before heading out to the barn. Royal did need a good, hard gallop. That was no lie. But Bree had failed to say where they were going.

She was going to ride right onto the Boot Knockers Ranch and demand to see Ty.

* * * * *

Royal was finicky today. She didn't want to wear the bit and she kept dancing sideways, shoving Bree against the wall of the barn.

"Are you mad at me, girl?" Bree looked her in the eye. "I was gone and no one loved you enough? I'm sorry." She stroked the horse's mane and rested her forehead against her neck. "I know the feeling. I missed…"

She swallowed that sentence, tried to forget the man it was about and saddled Royal.

Slipping into the saddle felt good, and galloping, better. She raced across the field, hunched small in her saddle to get more speed. She was feeling a little reckless and giddy.

Ty was within reach.

When she got to the ridge, the fence was in perfect repair and not a Roberts man was in sight. She led Royal in a wide circle, getting up speed for a jump. They'd made higher leaps but never had one felt so important. It was as if she were crossing a bridge. From youth to adulthood. From her old life to a new one.

No matter what happened with Ty, she would come back changed because she planned to tell him how she couldn't get him out of her head.

She spurred her horse and they sailed over the barbed wire. When they hit the ground, Royal shot downward, racing toward the valley and the buildings with red roofs.

The wind teased Bree's hair off her hot face and slithered into her neckline against her hot skin.

Once they hit flat turf, she slowed Royal. Two cowboys watched her ride in, tipping their hats in greeting. As she passed, she heard one say "Roberts girl".

Nobody stopped her. Not even when she rode into the middle of the buildings and dismounted.

"Hey."

She turned to see a woman with short, blue hair walking toward her. Bree sucked in a breath. Crap, she was about to be kicked off again.

"You're one of this week's vacationers, aren't you? They're all in the auditorium. You'd better get in there if you want to get your cowboy."

"Oh. Okay. Thanks." Bree tethered Royal to a post outside the barn with a trough filled with oats and water nearby.

Heart thumping, she went toward the auditorium. She'd heard rumors of how the women were selected by the Boot Knockers, but she'd never asked Ty.

She jerked to a stop. Ty was in there choosing another woman. A woman who would rake her nails over his hard, chiseled buns.

Oh hell no. Those buns were hers. Bree hurried forward and wrenched open the heavy door. Shadows swallowed her.

The cowboys were lined up in the leather chairs at the front of the building, the stage lit. As she moved down the center aisle, Bree kept her gaze on the woman in the spotlight. She was tall and had an earthy quality — she oozed sex appeal with her big hips and breasts and curly, long hair.

The woman's voice projected through the speakers as she spoke into the microphone. "I'm here because I want to find out how to make a body match."

"Can you explain what you mean by 'body match', Miss Rowena?" someone drawled.

Bree's lungs burned. That was Ty. Ty was asking this woman questions. Did that mean he was interested in her? That he'd have her in his bed all week, screaming for release the way he'd made Bree scream?

"In old times, people looked at each other and lusted. They fell into the weeds and got pleasure from each other without constraints of dating or marriage. They liked what they saw so they took it. That's a body match," Rowena explained.

Several cowboys bobbed their heads.

"Sounds mighty fine to me," Ty drawled.

Not. Happening.

Bree took off running. She sprinted past the line of cowboys and several women who stood along the sides in the shadows. Planting her hands on the stage, she vaulted and scrambled to her feet.

"What the—?" someone said.

"Where'd she come from?"

"She's not on my list," a woman said, rustling papers.

Bree stormed up to Rowena and shoved her aside. "I'm Bree and I'm looking for a body match too."

"Fuck," she heard Ty grate out. She squinted against the beam of lights and caught movement on the edge of the stage. Then she zeroed in on the big cowboy.

No, the big angry *cowboy.* Ty's body rolled with muscle as he leaped up and crossed the stage, head lowered like a bull prepared to charge.

Bree's fingers tingled. Maybe this wasn't such a good idea.

She backed up.

"Don't you dare try to run from me, woman."

Heat wove low through her pussy and made her nipples bunch. She couldn't draw enough air.

God, it was so good.

His boots thudded on the wooden floor. She took another step backward. And another. When she came up against a wall of curtain, she swallowed a squeak.

With a growl, Ty was on her. He caught her around the thighs and hoisted her over his shoulder. She grunted as his steely shoulder met her soft stomach. He brought his hand down on her ass cheek—hard.

"Ow!"

His stinging slap and her scream resounded through the big space as Ty carried her offstage, her legs dangling and her ass hoisted into the air for all to see.

Shameful.

And exciting.

He was steaming mad. She could feel it scorching her. For once she worried she'd pushed him too far. He could throw her off the ranch and never speak to her again. His indifference would kill her.

They broke into the open air and he swung her down. Her feet went out from under her and her backside crashed into the turf. She glared up at him. "Damn you!"

"No," he said in a deadly calm tone that worried her more than the fury in his eyes, "damn *you*, Bree. You don't belong here. And you sure as hell don't belong in that auditorium."

"You were going to pick that woman with the big tits," she spat, shoving to her feet. She felt hot and disheveled and uncertain. He wasn't giving her that I'm-going-to-spank-you-then-eat-you-up stare. It was more like a you've-fucked-up-my-life stare.

She swallowed as his eyes darkened another shade. "I was *supposed* to pick that woman with the big tits. It's my job, Bree."

"A sick job. I bet your parents are so proud."

"It's none of your business what I choose to do. This is my life and I won't have a spoiled little girl fucking it up."

"That's me? A spoiled little girl?"

He crowded close enough that his hard chest brushed the peaks of her aching breasts. Brackets were carved around his mouth and fire lit his eyes. "You know you are."

"You like it," she taunted.

He dipped his gaze to her mouth then back up. "There's a time and place for that sort of play, and you chose wrong. Get off the ranch, Bree."

She quivered. The uncertainty inside her snowballed into a monster. She clenched her fists.

"Go." His tone was so final, so dead. Something broke inside her.

"Please," she whispered. "I had to see you. I know you came looking for me at home. I thought…"

"You thought wrong." He jabbed a finger toward the auditorium. "You could have just cost me my job."

"It might be worth it."

"No."

She had to change his mind, to soften him and make him look at her the same way he had before…

Before she'd acted like an idiot. She dropped her gaze to her dusty boots.

"I screwed up. I shouldn't have interfered with your work. I just lost my head a little when I thought you were going to have that woman in your bed." Her voice trailed off until it was barely audible.

His chest rose and fell against hers, and his cinnamon-scented breath filled her with longing. "I oughta tie you up and spank you until you can't sit down for a week." His voice pitched low, fingers that teased her senses.

Her gaze locked on his and she saw it— that fire. The want. The absolute I'm-going-to-rule-you look that she couldn't get enough of.

She jumped in his arms. He hitched her legs around his waist and slammed his mouth into hers. Dark want burrowed deep in her pussy, and her panties flooded. She angled her head and threw herself into kissing him as he started walking.

Her heart rejoiced. This was what she'd come here for—once again Ty had given her everything she needed.

"God, I missed you," he growled as he paused. He shifted and wood banged—a door kicked open.

She scraped her teeth over his tongue, drawing a moan from him. His cock pressed against her pussy, rock-hard. She pushed against him.

"You're gonna pay for this, Bree. Pay big." He strode through the bunkhouse and tossed her on his cot. It creaked as he followed her down, cloaking her with his body.

Her mind and heart soared. Ty was hers, and he was about to prove it.

* * * * *

With a flick of his wrist he unbuckled his belt and yanked it free of the loops. When he folded it in half, Bree's eyes widened.

"What are you going to do with that?"

"What I shoulda done weeks ago. I'm going to spank your ass and send you away."

"You wouldn't." Her voice shivered.

Dammit, he should go through with his threat, but she was so fucking gorgeous and soft and *wanting*.

He grabbed her hip and flipped her onto her side. With her skintight jeans still covering her sensitive skin, he wouldn't hurt her.

Much.

He smiled grimly. Then delivered two sound whacks with the belt. She arched but didn't make a noise.

Damn her. There wasn't an ounce of fight, only sweet, giving female.

He tossed his belt to the floor and flipped her onto her back again. When he crushed his lips to hers, she mewled. He plunged his tongue into her mouth, too aware of how damn much he'd missed her.

She grappled at his shirt buttons then slid her silky hands over his chest. As she tweaked his nipples, he shoved his cock against the V of her legs. The need to control was still there, but somehow she was controlling him just as much. When had it happened? She acted out, he reacted. She needed, he gave.

He stripped her hastily, plucking her ripe nipples with his teeth, punishing her in a brand-new way.

As she scraped her nails over his shoulders, he fought a condom on one-handedly. The instant it was in place, he drove into her clenching heat.

Rearing back, he roared with satisfaction. She'd stopped him from doing his job but he was getting so much more. He'd said she needed the personal connection in bed, but he craved it just as much.

She locked her ankles behind his back, and they began to move. Holding her gaze, he pulled his length through her tight walls. Her eyes were wide, her lips swollen and her jaw red from his day-old beard scruff.

"You came down here and interrupted me for this, isn't that right, baby girl?" He panted between syllables.

She bucked upward, taking him deeper. They shared a groan. "I love you, Ty. I couldn't let another woman have you."

They stopped dead.

Had she just said the L-word? Jesus, he was a dead man because her words had burrowed into his soul.

He thrust hard and deep, shoving her up the cot until she had to hold on to the top to keep from falling off. Whatever they'd been doing together, it was so fucking perfect. Maybe not for everyone, but for them it was like finding the key that slid into a lock.

She loves me. He'd worry about his mind's war with his heart later. Right now he was going to make the woman that loved him scream with release.

Reaching between their bodies, he found her straining nubbin. He rocked it side to side under his fingertip. Her pussy contracted once, and he knew she was so close.

"Don't come until I tell you to, Bree. From now on, you don't do anything without thinking what I want first. You got it?"

Hell, she was getting off on his words. Her pupils were blown wide, her breathing coming fast and rough.

He flicked her clit, watching her face spasm with pleasure. His orgasm wasn't far away, and he couldn't afford to toy with her long. He'd blow it if he teased her much more.

Leaning over her, he took her mouth in a tongue-dueling kiss that snapped the last thread of his control. He plowed into her, taking, giving, a push and pull of power that sent him spurting with a roar.

She came apart around him, twitching in his hold. Her tongue tasting of tears and greed.

"Baby girl," he rasped almost in prayer.

* * * * *

Bree held herself rigidly in Ty's embrace. He was still panting after almost shoving her off the cot with every sexy, bone-melting thrust. He'd been out of control—and she'd loved every minute.

Except now she felt like the dumbest, silliest little girl ever. She'd told a man who had sex for a living that she loved him. How many others must have told him that after a week of experiencing his talents?

Rowena's words came to mind. *Body match.* He fucked lots of women, and lust probably fueled him as much as his duty to the ranch. He'd come to Bree for a different reason—she annoyed him. He'd probably slept with her to shut her up and in hopes that she'd eventually get her fill and go away.

And she'd just told him she loved him.

She pulled herself from under his big body and rolled off the cot. He cocked an eye open as she bent to gather her clothes. One of her boots was in plain sight but the other had gone missing. She searched for a long minute before she found it under the neighboring bunk.

"Where are you going?" His words sounded slurred. Each one lured her back.

But, no, she had to get out of there. This time she wouldn't come back. At least she had Royal and could be off the ranch in a hurry.

"Got work to do. Going home." She tugged on her jeans and fastened them. Her shirt followed. By the time she was dressed, he was sitting up, reaching for her.

"Don't go." He slipped his arms around her hips and dropped his head to her chest. Love swallowed her and for a moment she couldn't speak around the knot in her throat.

Everything about him was right. From his mussed hair to his long, bare feet. *This is gonna hurt.*

Stepping back, she hardened herself. "You're right, Ty. I don't belong here."

He stared at her, confusion etched on his rugged features. She couldn't shake the feeling he knew why she was going but waited for her to say it. He knew how to make her do and say things she didn't think possible. Well, he couldn't make her say she loved him a second time—or admit how stupid it was of her to have said it in the first place.

"I've gotta go."

"Bree."

"No, Ty." Words hung unsaid between them. Ty was smart and funny and he knew just how to anchor her when she was feeling adrift. All of those things had made her fall for him, but she'd get over it. He wasn't going to leave his job for her.

She spun and walked outside.

He followed, buck-ass naked, catching her arm. She looked at him in all his glory, that lost-little-boy look on his face, and almost threw her arms around him again.

No. She had to be the first to walk away. He'd inevitably deny her love and send her away for good. Then she'd crumble. Right now she was strong enough to do this.

He didn't even respond when I said I love him.

That hurt most. She'd said it and he hadn't even given her a man grunt.

Her cheeks heated and she yanked her arm away. "Hope you're not in too much trouble, Ty."

With that, she took off running, tearing around buildings, ignoring the cowboys walking through the grounds with their women of the week. As she approached Royal, her horse's whinny was balm to her aching soul. She untied the horse and launched onto her back.

Angling up the ridge toward home, she refused to let a single tear fall. She was strong and she hadn't come here for an attachment anyway. She was too young to settle down, but it sucked that her first love was completely unavailable.

* * * * *

What the hell just happened? Ty sat on his bunk for what felt like hours, his head in his hands. He was still reeling from Bree getting on that stage and demanding his time. He was also stunned by his own passion—a tornado force he'd never expected.

Especially after she'd admitted her feelings.

Tenderness rose inside him, a warm pool around his heart. He scuffed his hands over his face, making a rasping noise.

"Sorry. I didn't know anyone was in here." The familiar voice brought Ty out of his haze. He stood to face Elliot.

Elliot dipped his gaze over Ty, obviously noting he only wore jeans and hadn't bothered to buckle his belt after Bree left.

"You aren't interrupting me if that's what you're thinking," Ty said quietly.

Elliot's gaze skittered away. "We were all in the auditorium, man. You took Bree out on your shoulder."

"Yeah, well…she isn't here now."

"What's going on with her, really?" Elliot set a hand low on his hip.

Ty chanced a look at him. At least he wasn't wearing his emotions. Ty wouldn't be able to face his hurt, knowing he'd put it there. "I don't know what's going on with her."

Elliot nodded. "Fair enough."

"She had nothing to do with us, Elliot."

Elliot met his gaze and nodded. "That's partly why I'm here. To apologize for treating you like shit when you didn't return my feelings."

"I'm sorry. For all of it. I didn't mean to toy with you. I thought it was casual."

Elliot wore his concern. "I'm also here as your friend. You can talk to me about Bree if you want."

"I… Thanks. I'm not sure what to even think about her."

"Well, when you figure it out, I'm here for you."

Ty took a few steps toward him. Outstretching his hand, he grasped Elliot's.

Time to move on to another chapter of our friendship.

"Forgiven?" Ty ducked his head to catch Elliot's gaze.

A begrudging smile teased the corner of Elliot's lips. "You probably think I'm an idiot, falling for Jack then you."

"No. I think you want more of a connection than you get on a daily basis here."

"I'd better stop looking for it, I guess." He tapped the floor with a boot, as if stamping the idea into his own head.

"Don't lose who you are." Ty took a chance and put his arms around Elliot. Their embrace was strong, healing the gulley between them. When Ty released him, Elliot looked a fraction stronger.

"Hugh said if I ran into you, I was supposed to tell you it's your week off. He didn't sound too happy," Elliot said.

"I can imagine."

Just what he didn't want—to be the unreliable Boot Knocker. He was slipping—bad. All because of Bree.

Feeling better about his situation with Elliot at least, Ty got dressed and left the bunkhouse. Elliot moved toward the bungalows and his waiting female. As Ty watched Elliot's long legs carry him away, he couldn't bring himself to feel bad that he'd lost his chance to work this week after carrying Bree offstage.

Damn her. She was a pain in the ass. One that had reached into his chest and tugged his heartstrings with her confession.

Somehow he'd had two people fall for him in a short time. It boggled him. One person he'd let go, and Bree...she'd fled.

Pushing out a breath, Ty grabbed a shovel and headed toward the manure pile. What he needed was manual labor and there was always shit to shovel. He dug in and worked until the pile was lower and the wagon was full. Then he jumped on the tractor, hooked it to the full wagon and headed up the hill with it. Then he shoveled some more, spreading it over a plot of ground as fertilizer.

The sun beat down. Sweat beaded and he stripped off his shirt. Biceps burning, he set the point of his shovel into the earth and leaned on it. When he swiped away some sweat with his forearm, he focused on his tattoo. The ace of spades. Once his winning card. He'd played the game of life and ended up on the Boot Knockers Ranch because of a poker game. Winning hand, he was taking the position Hugh had offered. Losing and he'd become a professor to satisfy his mother.

Then he'd turned over the ace of spades. He'd never looked back.

Until now.

He pivoted and looked up the ridge toward the Roberts ranch. Bree's leaving was no good. Not because he didn't want her to go—it was about time the little vixen realized she didn't belong here.

She'd gone without a sass or a backward glance. She'd told him she loved him then climbed out of his bed. Why?

He tore into the manure wagon again. His mouth was parched, but he ignored his needs as he tried to figure out what the hell Bree had really needed. He should know—he'd worked with countless females, and it wasn't all about sex. He talked to them, learned their hopes and fears. Listened to their stories that eventually gave him insights as to how to help them.

For a while he'd believed he'd figured out Ms. "Feisty Pants" Roberts. She needed to be sweet and giving for the right man. Ty had broken down some wall and she'd let him in—into her heart.

Damn. He didn't want to be evicted from that special space. He wanted to sink his roots deep and build a foundation.

He stopped. The shovel dropped from his hands and he stared toward the ridge.

When had it happened? Sometime between him growling commands and having her soft and begging, he'd allowed her into *his* heart too.

He backhanded his eyes. Damn.

He slid his boot under the shovel handle and lifted it into his hands again. But ten shovelfuls only convinced him that he couldn't leave things as they were.

Fifteen more and he came to the conclusion that it was a good thing he couldn't work with a client this week. Ten more and he knew he'd be worthless next week too.

He threw down the shovel and hopped on the tractor. While he drove back to the outbuilding and then stored the farm equipment, he thought of how to word his request to his bosses.

All those words fled the minute he stood in Hugh's office with the big oak desk between them.

"Jeezus, not again." Hugh raked his fingers through his hair.

Riggs entered from a room in the rear, curiosity on his dark features. "Is this about Elliot?"

"No." Ty danced from foot to foot.

"Just say it," Hugh demanded.

"Elliot and I are fine. We made amends a little bit ago."

"Good to hear." Riggs nodded and came around to lean against Hugh's desk, positioned between Ty and Hugh, acting as a buffer.

Ty swallowed. "I'd like to request leave."

Hugh turned to stone. He didn't move—blink, shift, breathe, itch his nose or fart. His gaze leveled on Ty, and while his eyes were hollow, Ty felt as if he were under the gaze of a pharaoh. A mummified king in a gold coffin who still evoked fear after thousands of years.

He shook himself and Hugh came to life. He tapped his thick finger against his lips. "I have to admit, you've blindsided me, Ty. I was so distracted by the Elliot saga I didn't even see this coming."

"What?"

"This is about the Roberts girl."

"Yes. No. Maybe not."

"Which is it?"

"I dunno. I need the time to figure it out."

"You realize you signed a contract stating you wouldn't get involved in a relationship outside of those on the ranch?" Hugh sounded like a lawyer and Ty was on the witness stand.

"I do." He straightened. "But life is sometimes messier than the words that are used to constrain it."

Riggs gave a crooked smile then shot Hugh a look. "I forgot he was a valedictorian."

"Yes, and he's one of our best damn cowboys on this ranch."

They were discussing Ty as if he weren't standing there. He spoke up. "I can be that again. I just need some time to get my head on straight."

"And what if your head's always cocked north toward the Roberts place?" Hugh waved toward Ty's crotch.

He met his boss's gaze. Hugh was more than a boss, though. He was a friend—a friend who'd done this same thing. Fallen for a woman—and man—who didn't fit into the wording on the contract.

"That may be the case, but I promise to give you notice if it is."

"Five days." Hugh sat back in his big leather chair, arms folded. "You've got five days to figure out what you're doing. I can't afford more."

"You got it. Thanks." Ty shook Riggs's hand, then Hugh's. Respect for his bosses was echoed in their expressions. So when Ty left the office, got in his truck and headed up the ridge, he felt a measure of peace.

At last.

* * * * *

The screen door banged behind Bree as she backed out of the house, holding the bucket of food slop for the pigs. She didn't regularly feed the few pigs they raised for food but Cook was looking a little more tired than usual and Bree had offered.

Carrying the heavy bucket of parings and scraps across the turf, she squinted against the tiny pellets of rain striking her face. It didn't rain frequently but when it did, it was usually the hard, pounding variety that brought high winds and lightning. It wasn't often she could enjoy cool rain on her face.

And she seriously needed it after the night she'd had. Tossing in bed until well past three, thinking of Ty and what they'd done together. Replaying their first meeting all the way to her final look at him. The man never did anything by halves—he'd even followed her out of the bunkhouse buck naked.

While his chiseled body was etched in her memory forever, his confused expression was a stake in her heart. Was he really so clueless that he hadn't realized her reason for leaving?

Maybe so. Her girlfriends—and even her cousin—said men didn't have the same way of thinking as women. After her college roommate's last breakup, she'd called men chickens, so stupid they'd turn around and eat their own droppings. That was a jaded view of the male species Bree didn't share.

But her cousin's words were a little fresher in her mind after spending those weeks in Omaha.

"If he hasn't realized how good you are, you make him see."

"And if that doesn't work?"

"Then you walk away and see if he comes to his senses."

Good advice, except Ty hadn't wanted her in the first place.

But he'd given her everything she'd ever needed. Somehow he'd known what those things were.

Not this time.

Bree rounded the corner of the barn and caught movement at the chicken coop. A dog had his head in the open door.

"Hey! Get outta there." The animal she'd raised from a pup didn't respond to her order. She strode toward the coop.

Then the reason the coop door was open emerged—all six foot two of him.

She stopped so fast the contents of the slop bucket spilled over onto her fingers. "Shit."

Ty.

Her heart lodged in her throat, pounding a wild tattoo.

He looked her over nice and slow, from boots to the tips of her hair follicles. Everything between scorched, pinched, hardened or grew slick. His gaze flicked to her messy fingers.

"Be careful the pigs don't bite off your fingers when you dump that slop in," he drawled.

A growl rose in her throat, replacing her heart. She had an urge to slosh the contents over his damn handsome face.

"Just what are you doing cleaning my chicken coop?"

"Boss said it needed doing."

She sputtered and almost dropped the bucket. "Boss?"

"Yeah, your pa. He hired me on."

"When?" Blood beat in her temples. What the hell was going on?

"Last night." A chicken pecked at the leg of his jeans but he didn't nudge it away as she sometimes did. It should be attacking him. Even the chickens were traitors.

And Daddy.

She glared at Ty. The man looked as out of place here as an albino on the surface of the sun. "You aren't a hand."

"Am now."

"For how long?"

He took a step toward her, and she backed up as his heat washed over her skin. Her senses dulled as he overwhelmed her with his scent and big muscles. And that burning look was in his eyes—the one he wore before he devoured her.

She took another step backward.

"For as long as it takes, baby girl."

"I...don't understand." She didn't like feeling vulnerable in his presence. How was she ever going to harden her heart against him when he showed up in her life, on her ranch? Doing her chores?

"You know why I'm here, Bree."

She whirled, slopping more sticky stuff over her fingers, and strode away. Chest burning, she waited for him to overtake her, to demand she look at him.

Or put my ass in the air.

Her skin pebbled as if reaching for his touch.

"No," she muttered, practically running to the pigpen. When she stepped on the lower rail of the fence and dumped the slop into the hog's trough, she stole a look around. No Ty.

Turmoil bubbled inside her. What game was he playing now?

Who was she kidding? She loved his games.

But not this one. She needed distance and he hadn't respected that. He'd barged onto her ranch and asked her daddy for a job. He did what he wanted — when he wanted. Damn if it didn't turn her on.

Water trickled over her spine, colder and wetter than the light rain. She jumped down and spun —

And was struck in the face by a spray of hose water.

Her nerve endings jumped to attention.

"What are you doing?" she screamed.

"Washing you off before…" His drawl was a lick to her flesh.

"Before what?" She spit out a mouthful of water and turned her head aside. He let the water stream over her breasts, molding the fabric to their curves.

"Before I punish you for being mouthy." He cut the water and dropped the hose. Came forward. Each roll of muscle ignited her. Her knees sagged, ready to submit.

She steeled her muscles and shook her head. With as much command as she could muster with a cowgirl's version of a wet plaid-shirt contest, she glared at Ty. "You don't run things up here."

"No? I think I have command over you no matter where you are."

A finger of need teased her pussy but she ignored it and the dark promise in his eyes. "I don't belong to you."

"Your body says differently. I see your nipples pointing right at me, begging me to suck them."

He couldn't talk to her like this. Anyone could hear them and —

Damn, she wanted him to shove her against the hog barn and make her a boneless puddle.

Well, maybe not the hog barn.

She threw the bucket at him. It bounced off his shin and rolled several feet from his boot. Quivering, she plastered her spine to the fence, waiting for his displeasure.

Aching for it.

What kind of twisted game were they playing?

Whatever it is, I want it. Need it.

"You want to try that again, baby girl?" He came forward, worn jeans pulling tight over his thighs and bulge evident between them.

"No." How she'd made her voice that strong was beyond her. She could barely breathe.

He bore down on her, but before he crushed his chest to her throbbing nipples and his mouth to hers, she shoved him back. With a sliver of space between them, she ducked and ran. From behind, she heard him call, "You forgot your bucket."

But she broke toward the house and the refuge of her room. She had to get away from a man who made her feel so off-balance and freaking amazing that she'd do anything for him. If she couldn't have all of him, what good was the amazing sex and their mindfucks?

She'd wanted nothing more than for him to leave his job and chase her, to love her enough to do that. So why was she pushing him away? Was she testing the strength of his decision, trying to see if he'd leave her?

A hot shower didn't ease her panic and neither did icy cold. So she threw herself on her bed, wrapped in a fluffy robe, and tried to make sense of her bucking emotions and Ty's presence.

When the lunch bell sounded, she groaned. She couldn't face him at the table with her ranch family surrounding them. They'd know what was going on, even if Ty *did* behave. They'd all known Bree long enough to be aware when something was wrong.

A light tap on her door. She got up and stared at the slab, heart thundering. Holding her breath, she opened it.

"Your father sent me to fetch you for lunch." God, he was delicious, disheveled and dirty.

"I heard the bell," she snapped at Ty. What the hell? He was coming to her room and her father *knew* it? They'd rounded the bend of crazy and were barreling straight into batshit nuts.

"Then I expect to see you seated across from me in two minutes, Bree."

Her head fell back. The sound of his voice sent spikes of need through her all over again.

For thirty seconds she stared at the door, wondering what he'd do to her if she didn't listen. Wondering what he'd do to her if she did.

"Son of a..." She threw off her robe and rushed into a set of clothes. With hair damp and trailing over her shoulders, she took her seat at the long table, wedged between the foreman and a ranch hand.

Directly across from Ty.

Beneath the table, the toe of his boot depressed hers.

As she met his gaze, love bloomed in her soul.

* * * * *

If Ty didn't get his hands on Miss "Hellion" Roberts soon, he was going to combust. In the past twenty-four hours he'd seen Bree at meals, in the fields and strutting in shorts the size of a postage stamp. The other guys had noticed too, which had nearly caused Ty to crack a tooth grinding them.

Also the clock was ticking and if he didn't get her to come around soon, he'd be back on the Boot Knockers Ranch, doing a job he no longer liked very well.

How had things changed so quickly? Hell if he knew, but he wasn't going to go against his instinct now. Not where Bree was concerned.

He stripped off his shirt and stuffed the tail into his back pocket. For some reason the Roberts ranch felt ten degrees hotter than the Boot Knockers Ranch in the valley. Maybe because the breeze was deflected off the mile-long stretch of Roberts trees and funneled into the valley. Or maybe it had everything to do with Bree.

As he worked through his chores, he settled into a rhythm. It wasn't exactly work befitting his degree, but he wasn't there to run the ranch. He started around the corner, his mind on a cool glass of sweet tea.

He looked up just as a body slammed into him.

"Oomph!"

He caught her, fingers wrapping around supple curves. She blinked up at him, appearing dazed.

He skimmed a finger over her plump lower lip, hunger erasing thoughts of anything but her. She wrenched free of his hold. Silken strands of hair tumbled into her blazing eyes.

"Don't you know you aren't on your ranch anymore? Ranch hands wear shirts," she snapped.

"I'm feeling mighty hot, Bree."

"It's not respectable." Was it him or did she sound a bit breathless?

"No one's around to see."

She sank her teeth into her lower lip and he bit off a groan. Too well he remembered how sharp those pearly whites were. He hardened.

She whirled away and flounced across the yard to the barn. "I've got animals to see to."

"Oh?"

"Daddy asked me to check on a few cows we have split off." Pride burned in her pretty features. His breath caught.

"I'm going with you."

"Oh hell no."

He almost laughed. Then she disappeared into the barn and came out with her mare saddled. He jerked his arms into his sleeves, letting his shirt hang open. She edged her horse so close to him that he rocked back.

Grabbing her round thigh, he looked up into her face. "Wait for me."

"Just try to catch me," she cooed. Spurring her horse, she darted off.

He ran for the nearest mount and was after her in seconds. God, she was gorgeous, leaning over her horse's neck, racing across the field. Her hair streamed out behind and her heart-shaped ass in the saddle spurred him faster.

When he caught her, he was going to—

His heart seized as she flipped over the side of her horse. "Yaw!" He dug his heels into his mount's side, terror freezing his fingers.

She hung off. She was going to fall and be dragged. Maybe killed.

With heart thumping in time to his horse's hooves, he pushed harder.

She flipped again, rolling upright in her saddle, riding with the perfect posture of an English lady.

What the fuck?

He no sooner blinked and she flipped off the other side, legs pointed straight toward the dark blue sky.

"Damn trick rider," he ground out. Wait until he got her bare ass under his hand. He'd let her know that scaring him wasn't a good idea.

By the time she did the fourth trick, his heart had resumed a normal beat. But when she stood in the saddle, he almost lost it.

Because she'd slowed a little, he caught up. She rode alongside him, shooting him a sideways glance.

"You break your pretty neck and I'll make you pay."

She laughed, the sound caught on the wind. Sounding like summer and picnics and all the good things in life. She eased down into the saddle with all the grace of a professional ballerina.

He didn't know what to say. She moved him, made him want to be a better man. To have more just to give it all to her.

In silence they rode up to a group of cows. A small herd, freshly branded by the looks of it.

"New cattle?" he asked.

She circled the group and back toward him. "Yes, quarantined."

His brows shot up. "Why?"

"Couple died two days ago. Daddy had a vet up here but he didn't know the cause of death."

"Where'd they come from? Might have been travel stress."

"We don't think so. Daddy thought it best to keep them away from the rest of the herd, so they were brought here. Help me count."

A minute later they said at the same time, "Fifty-six."

She smiled, stabbing him in the heart like sun to the eyes of a man too long in darkness.

He wet his lips. "Is that the right number?"

"Yes. We haven't lost any."

"Good." He snagged her reins and yanked her horse to a stop. Then he pulled her right out of the saddle and into his arms. She thumped against his groin, her ass nestled against his hard-on, her lips close.

"Ty." Her voice was a warning but her body quivered.

"Ride with me. Let's just talk." He settled her into the saddle before him, leaving her horse to crop grass as they trotted in a leisurely pace across the field.

He placed his lips near her ear. "Favorite toy as a child?"

She turned her head, placing her delicious lobe right between his teeth. He bit down gently, and she burrowed closer. "Uhh…a baby doll I called Jenny."

"Bet you took good care of her."

She giggled and writhed as he nibbled up the shell of her ear. "Not really. I cut off all her hair and left her in the rain."

"Bad girl." He pinched her ass, raising a gasp. God, he wanted to keep her panting under him all night long on sweaty, twisted sheets.

He kissed the sensitive spot on her throat, and she fell still. "Favorite meal?"

"Chicken and biscuits."

"Mmm. Good choice."

"What's yours?"

"Bree with a side of whipped cream."

"That's…" *pant, pant,* "…not a meal."

"It will be, I promise you."

"I thought we were…talking." Her breathing hitched as he swirled his tongue over the column of her throat, flicking down into her open shirt collar. He loved her in ranch attire. All buttoned up and wearing everything but spurs, she was more tantalizing. Maybe because he knew what was underneath all that fabric.

"We *are* talking, baby girl. Where do you see yourself in five years?"

"What — is this a job interview?"

"Answer the question."

She was silent for so long he grew concerned enough to stop sucking her neck and turn her face to look at him.

"You don't know, do you?" he asked.

Her eyes were too bright. With tears? Damn, he didn't want to upset her.

"No," she whispered.

"That's okay. You know why?"

"Why?"

"Because I don't know either. That doesn't mean we can't do great things together." The emotions he had for her needed more time to settle in his mind. He needed to see where they fit into his life — and hers.

She stiffened until he thought she'd shatter. "Take me back to my horse, Ty."

"Bree — "

"Take me back."

Feeling the change in her and the electricity that fizzled out, he sighed and grabbed the reins. Maybe he'd done the wrong thing in coming here. Maybe all they had was the sexual chemistry and talking didn't work. Getting to know each other was a dead end.

Didn't she understand how much he cared, just by how hard he was trying to get to know her?

At least by day five he'd have a better sense of whether their relationship could be more or he needed to prowl the bungalows again, making other women smile.

As he watched Bree gallop ahead of him the whole way home, all he could think was how bad he wanted this to work. But how to loosen her without a spanking?

Chapter Twelve

Flames shot into the air, tickling the sky with orange sparks. As Bree grew mesmerized by the bonfire and the low, rough voices of the men sitting around it, something nudged her ankle. She looked down to see one of her favorite barn cats.

She bent and scooped it under its plump stomach, cradling the fuzz ball against her chest. "What are you doing out here? You should be in your bed."

The cat pawed at her and she scratched its ears. Then she moved around the outer circle of men, looking for an open stump to pull up to the fire and enjoy the social gathering.

A big hand came out of the darkness and clamped around her wrist. She looked down at the hand and followed the hard knuckles to a strong arm spattered with dark hair, and all the way up to the man.

Her heart squeezed.

"Sit with me," Ty said.

Somehow he'd managed to snag one of the half logs for a seat, rather than the upright stumps. And since this wasn't the Boot

Knockers Ranch, there was little chance of two cowboys cozied up side by side.

Bree hesitated and the cat pawed at her again.

Ty reached up and closed his hands around the animal, bringing it into his lap. With a thumping heart, Bree took the seat. Immediately the cool of the night fled. Between the raging fire and Ty at her side, she was toasty warm. The urge to lean against him was strong but she resisted.

She couldn't give in to his nearness. It was so easy to slip into his arms and close her eyes while he stroked her spine with those perfectly rough fingers, but that couldn't happen ever again.

She'd been there, done that, and she'd had the wet panties to prove it.

The ranch foreman was talking, but it wasn't about work. He was a great storyteller and sometimes Bree came here just to listen to him. She'd grown up around most of these men and they all felt like family. Secretly she'd believed her father would want her to marry one of these hardworking men to help carry on the legacy of the Roberts ranch, but she wasn't sure.

Daddy *had* given Ty a job. Maybe...

Movement beside her caught her attention and she grew entranced by Ty's hands moving over the cat he held. With every stroke, the tabby stretched and arched. Bree had never wanted to be a cat so much in her life.

Of course, if she inched closer to Ty, he'd put his hands on her too. Heat coiled low in her belly, creating a satisfying ache between her legs. As she listened to the foreman, she felt herself leaning toward the solid wall of muscle beside her.

Her sleeve brushed his arm and she snapped upright.

He gave her a crooked smile that ratcheted up her desire tenfold. So easy to cuddle against him and listen to the stories of great-grandfathers who had shaped Texas into the land as they knew it.

Several men grunted greetings and she stiffened her spine as her father entered the ring and took a stump. His gaze searched her out right away. Ty gave her daddy a nod and let the cat slip to the ground. It padded off into the night.

Someone was passing a flask. It reached her and she took a deep pull. Then another.

"Have a third sip, baby girl. I'd like to see you lose your inhibitions," Ty rumbled low enough only she could hear.

"You want to take advantage of me."

"Hell yeah. You know I didn't come to work here for the great view and to learn the ropes."

His words lassoed her heart, tugging too hard for her sanity. One more word would be the strong pull that sent her tumbling. He'd come here for her. But why? Did it have to do with her admitting her feelings?

Panting around the burn of the whiskey, she passed the flask to Ty. He didn't take a single sip, just handed it to the next guy several feet away.

The talk went on but Bree didn't follow it. Her mind was occupied with Ty. When he spoke, she burned.

"I knew a man like that once. A real hard-ass. He rodeoed for a while before he busted too many toes to make it comfortable to wear boots."

"That so?" someone asked.

"Yeah. They were all curled up-like and he was forced to wear orthopedic shoes."

Men laughed. "Imagine a cowboy in orthopedic shoes."

Ty shook his head, his grin wide and the creases around his eyes thickening Bree's throat. She wanted to lean in and trace them with her lips, down to the brackets around his mouth and then on to his stubbled jaw.

She shifted on the seat and he pegged her with a knowing gaze. The one that turned her to pudding.

"I always wondered how he'd get the spurs to attach to his shoes, ya know?" Ty's words roused more laughter. Bree stole another glance at him. He fit right in here. Even her father was laughing.

One man got up and dumped a lapful of peanut shells into the fire. The flames licked upward and the foreman chuckled. "Don't worry, Boss. You've got Cook in the kitchen and this cowpoke won't be taking over."

Her father's smile weakened a bit and his gaze met Bree's. They were thinking the same thing.

"I'm not sure our greenhorn knows the story about the fire of '96."

"No, probably not."

At the word "greenhorn", Ty perked up, listening.

Bree's brain started to hum. This story was legacy on the ranch but it hurt her to hear it. Whenever someone mentioned her mother, it raised good and bad emotions.

"I dunno if I'm the best person to tell that story. Bree was there."

"I was three years old, Daddy."

"Three years old? In '96? Hell, I had three wives by then," one ranch hand said to several guffaws.

Feeling heat infuse her face, Bree hunched her shoulders.

Ty's fingers crept across the bench and covered her hand where it was planted. She turned her head his way, finding their faces too close. His scent too good.

"Tell me the story," he said.

Pulling her hand into her lap, she tried to make sense of what she remembered and what she'd been told. After a minute, she figured it didn't matter. It was a campfire story and the guys would like it regardless.

"Momma never had a cook growing up, so she didn't want one when she took on my daddy." She inclined her head slightly toward her father, whose eyes looked suspiciously glassy. She went on before her own tears threatened.

"She knew how to cook, but not for thirty-odd cowboys with hollow legs."

More peanut shells made the fire flare once again.

"She was good at making hearty soups—stews and chili."

"Oh, her chili was the stuff that sticks to a cowboy's ribs!" a man added.

"And kept the rest of us up with yer farts," someone else said. More laughter and Ty's shoulders moved with his chuckle. Each brush against Bree shot new sparks through her body.

She took command. "This is my story. Am I telling it or are we talking about gas in the bunkhouse?"

Ty's gaze was on her, and she grew aware of how bratty she'd sounded. She folded her fingers and started again.

"Momma had a big kettle of turkey noodle soup on the stove. I don't remember this part, but I hear that I was a demanding little girl—"

"No!"

"I can't believe that."

"Never saw such a cute little thing, though," the foreman said.

She glanced at Ty. His face was unreadable, his gaze steady.

"I was screaming that I needed help with my cowgirl boots and Momma left the stove. Next thing you knew, the whole kitchen was on fire. Hands came running from all over the ranch at the sign of smoke. There was a bucket brigade."

"Then Bree went missing." Her father's words still echoed his fear from that day—fear she couldn't remember. She only recalled thinking the colors of the fire were so pretty. She'd been awed by its power as it licked up the walls after turning the corner and seeing it.

She held her breath. Maybe she'd always been drawn by forces bigger than she was. No wonder Ty drove her insane.

"They searched everywhere for me while about half the cowboys kept pouring water on the fire. Momma was frantic. I remember her face when she found me." Bree's voice cracked.

"Where were you?" Ty asked.

"'Round the corner pettin' the dog."

"Oblivious," her father interjected.

"I was too little to care. I was upset not to have turkey noodle soup, though. And about the drawings on the refrigerator that burned up. After that, Momma gave in and hired a cook."

Daddy's smile was soft, his gaze far off.

Ty leaned in until his mouth was a breath from Bree's ear. "You still miss her and honor her with your memories."

Her throat closed.

Warm fingers threaded under her hair, searching. When Ty discovered the velvety patch she kept shaven, her heart stopped.

"I know, Bree. All of it."

Because you know me.

Tears were too close. She jumped up and made a show of dusting her jeans. "I'm going to bed. Don't stay up too late, y'all."

She didn't make it past the barn before Ty overtook her. He caught her around the waist and she snapped her arm around his neck, lifting onto tiptoe as his lips crushed hers. The decadent scents of male and musk chiseled her resolve and bricks started to fall.

He worked his hand around her nape and under her hair, stroking back and forth over the spot she kept because of her mother. It made their kiss all the sweeter.

Angling her head, she parted her lips for his tongue. He didn't invade swift and hot, as she'd expected. Instead, he gently tangled his tongue with hers, tasting, searching. That damn L-word jumped into her head again. She tried to pull back but he wouldn't let her.

He hooked her leg high on his thigh and rocked slowly, rhythmically, maddeningly against her pussy. She flooded with want and something bittersweet lodged in her soul.

"Don't turn me away," he murmured between kisses.

It broke through her haze. Dropping her leg from his hip, she shoved back. He wouldn't let her go. He forced her gaze up to his.

"I'm not a Boot Knocker right now, Bree."

What did that mean? She stared at his eyes, so dark under the thin light of the moon. Rowdy laughter from the bonfire floated on the air, and Bree found the strength to disentangle herself from the man she loved.

He slipped his hands into his front pockets, head bowed, looking as dejected as she'd ever seen a man. She wanted to share more sweet kisses but she needed to get her head on straight.

"'Night, Ty."

He thumbed his hat. "'Night, baby girl."

As she walked back to the house, she couldn't ignore the slickness between her legs. Or the slow melt of her heart. She didn't know how much longer she could resist him.

* * * * *

Ty'd shoveled more in the time since he'd met Bree than he had since he was a boy. Seemed he was always trying to clear his head and manual labor helped.

Not enough.

He didn't know how to convince her that he was here to try to make a go of it. Of course, he wasn't good with expressing his emotions. She might not be getting what he was trying to convey. Did she need him to tell her he loved her? She was a smart girl. Surely she'd see that he'd left the job he'd loved — for her.

Last night their tender, unhurried kiss had felt like a milestone. In many ways their relationship was backward—they'd jumped right into sex before getting to know each other. The courting part needed to happen. At least that's what he thought, but there was no handbook for women. He knew a lot from his job, but none of those women were Bree.

"You're doing a hell of a job for me, greenhorn."

He looked over his shoulder at Bree's father. The man chewed on a sliver of grass in the corner of his mouth.

"Thank you, sir."

"I think you're more responsible for other changes around here, though."

"What do you mean?" Ty leaned on his shovel, sweating freely.

"My daughter. I see a difference in her."

Ty drew a deep breath and released it. "Good difference?"

"Yeah," he drawled as if he wasn't sure either. "She's softer somehow. More grown up."

"She isn't a child."

"No. But around you she acts like the woman I always knew she could be. A lot like her mother, actually."

Ty nodded. Bree had grown more serious and mature since even he'd met her. Their sex play had morphed into something adult and deep enough that they'd both grown. Now if Ty could convince her that he wanted that...

"Keep doing what you're doing and she'll come around."

Ty met his boss's gaze. "How can you be so sure?"

"Because she isn't only her mother's daughter. My blood runs in her veins and I know myself, Ty." He nodded toward the shovel. "Get back to work."

His words were overlaid by shouts. A horse and rider tore around the corner. "Come quick! It's Bree."

Ty dropped the shovel and ran with Dan Roberts at his side. His insides churned as he spotted the ranch hand on horseback prancing in agitation. Ty ran to the nearest corral, ripped the gate open and hurled himself onto the nearest horse. He gave it the spurs.

"Where?"

"This way! Royal went down." The rider whirled and took off. Dan shot past Ty on his own horse, and they thundered toward the distant field.

Ty set his lips in a fierce line as he imagined his baby girl sprawled under 900 pounds of animal, injured or worse. He kicked his horse faster.

The minute he spotted the hump of flesh on the ground, time slowed. Images of Bree flashed through his mind in rapid succession, a slideshow on superspeed. Her smile, her eyes when he entered her, her bound and at his mercy. And the way she'd looked last night after he'd told her he wasn't a Boot Knocker right now. Did she understand that he meant he wasn't acting, putting on a show? He was close to her because he'd chosen to be.

His horse skidded and he leapt off, boots digging into the turf. Bree lay on her side, coughing.

Punctured lung, broken ribs. Internal injuries. His brain shot through different diagnoses but he had no idea what he'd find. He ran to her side and dropped to his knees.

"Daughter." Dan hit his knees too and they both reached, united in their love for her.

Love.

Ty had to tell her.

She rolled onto her back, face smeared with dirt and grass clinging to her silky hair. "I'm...okay."

"Don't move too quick. You could have injured something and not realize it yet." Ty ran his hands over her sides, gently probing ribs and trim waist.

"Royal...hit a hole. She fell."

"You were standing in that saddle, weren't you?" Dan asked.

Her eyes were round. She blinked. "Does it matter? Royal—" She struggled into a sitting position, but Ty held her in place.

The horse lay on its side, chest heaving. Its eyes rolled in pain.

The ranch hand who'd seen her take the fall grabbed his rifle and started forward.

"No!" Bree's agony-filled voice spurred Ty into action.

He jumped up and clasped the rifle barrel. "Don't do it."

"Horse is hurt bad enough. You're only prolonging her pain."

Bree scrambled over to Royal's side and splayed her hands over her animal.

"I know a great horse specialist. The best, actually," Ty said.

"Where?" Dan barked.

"Boot Knockers Ranch. A woman lives on the far end of the valley a little up the ridge. New construction. Porch isn't finished," Ty spewed.

"Ride for her," Dan commanded.

The ranch hand was in the saddle and pounding away in seconds. Ty moved close to Bree, more worried about her than he could bear. He studied her pose, looking to see if she was favoring any body part, but she seemed okay.

She bent over her horse. Sobs racked her.

Ty met Dan's gaze then wrapped his arms around Bree. He kissed her cheek, tasting her salt, and smoothed her hair. "It's going to be okay, baby girl. Lissy's amazing. If anything can be done, she'll do it. Dan, we're going to need the vet too. His facilities and transport."

"I'll call now." He stepped away to make the call.

As Ty tended the horse, making her as comfortable as possible, he felt Bree's gaze on him.

"When I thought you might be injured, Bree—"

She cut him off with a wave of her hand. "Not now, Ty."

"Not now or not ever?"

Lissy's truck rolled into sight and Ty breathed a sigh of relief that she was there to soothe and care for the animal. The vet's transport rumbled through the field toward them next. Bree got to her feet. She looked right at Ty and tried to close an invisible door in his face. "Ever."

"I'm going to show you what happens when you don't believe in me."

Was that hope he saw in her eyes?

* * * * *

Exhaustion stole over Bree. After spending hours in the vet's waiting room in a stiff-backed chair waiting to hear whether or not Royal Hoofprints would make it through surgery, she could barely hold herself up.

She toweled off her hair and dragged her fingers through the damp locks, too tired to bother finding her hairbrush. Then she fell into bed, also too lazy to put on a nightgown or even panties. Her prized horse—one of her best friends in the world—had come out of anesthesia with no trouble and the sweet woman named Lissy had assured her the animal would make a full recovery.

Royal might not be into full-gallop mode for a while, but Bree's relief was huge. She sprawled on her stomach, face buried in her feather pillow.

The door banged off the inner wall and she twisted, shooting upward.

"Good. You're ready for me." Ty strode in and closed the door much more quietly than he'd opened it.

"What the hell are you doing? Get out!" She lashed an arm over her bare breasts and slapped the pillow over her pussy, but the way he looked at her set her on fire.

He took off his hat and tossed it. It struck a lamp and tipped it over. Uncaring, he approached the bed. "Get back into that position, baby girl."

Her tremble grew into a full-on quake. What was he going to do to her? And in her own bed with her father at the other end of the house? No, this couldn't happen.

"I'll keep you quiet," Ty said as if knowing her thoughts. He tugged a handkerchief from his back pocket and shook it out.

"I'm not doing anything with you. We're through, Ty."

"Like hell." He hooked a finger beneath her jaw and hovered with his lips inches from hers and eyes burning. "We haven't even started. Now face down."

She glared, lips set. "Go find someone else to play with."

"I don't want someone else. I want you."

A shiver snaked down her spine and warmth bloomed in her heart. Did he mean…?

He yanked the hanky around her mouth and knotted it so quickly she barely had time to blink. Shocked, she kicked at him. The insane cowboy reached behind him and produced a small loop of rope. He unfurled it and while she kicked and fought, getting wetter by the second, he flipped her onto her stomach and bound her ankle to the bedpost. Then the other.

She pushed onto her hands, angry and needy and so confused she couldn't have voiced it even if she weren't gagged.

"So fucking wet for me already," he rumbled. When he ran a fingertip over her wet folds, she almost buckled. Stiffening her arms, she steeled herself to withstand him. He didn't love her. This was a game to him. To them both at first, but she'd fallen in love with him along the way.

He didn't feel the same.

Did he?

I don't want someone else. I want you, he'd said.

He traced a path down her spine and over one buttock. It took everything in her not to arch like that barn cat under his touch.

"Put your arms out, Bree." His commands tripled her need.

When she didn't obey at once, he slapped her on the ass—hard. The crack resounded through her room. Pleasure-pain coiled in her system. She panted against the sheets, burning and wishing she weren't. She wanted him to love her back and if he didn't, she wanted out.

He was making it pretty damn difficult for her to walk away, though. He caressed the spot he'd just spanked. "Getting a nice shade of pink for me already. Before the night's over, I'm going to have both cheeks hot and red. When I sink into your tight pussy, you're going to feel every place I've touched you. And when I sink into your ass," he gripped each cheek, fingers biting into her deliciously, "I'm going to feel the heat I've created on your skin."

She shuddered, unable to stop herself from writhing. Slowly, she inched her hands over the bed until she was flat.

"Good girl." He tied her arms up and apart before sliding down the gag and bending to kiss her with so much emotion that she had to swallow a sob. When he pulled back, he put the gag back in her mouth. "When I'm finished teaching you whom you belong to, I'll take off the gag and we'll have a nice, long discussion. But if you don't want this, you can easily slip your hand free. See?"

He pulled off the rope and she flexed her fingers.

"Tap the bed three times and I'll know you want to stop. I'll always do what you want, in the end, baby girl."

Her response was muffled. He bound her wrist again. A second later she didn't care if she ever spoke again. He walked around the bed and eased his fingers up and down her creamy slit until she was on the verge of bliss. Juices drenched his fingers. The knot in her core tightened.

Then he moved away, leaving her cold and quivering. No longer angry, just needy and excited. When the quiet hum of her vibrator pierced the air, she jerked her bonds. Twisting, she tried to see him. Her skin prickled and a flush coated her cheeks.

He directed the vibrator at her center. Her hips lifted on their own, and he fitted the rubber against her swollen clit. She cried out, thankful for the gag.

"Here's where I tell you how it's gonna be, baby girl. I'm going to fuck you long and hard tonight. With this." He applied more pressure to her clit with the toy. She bucked. "And this." He took her foot and pressed it to something hard and bulging—his cock. She curled her toes around the denim, aching to feel him inside her. To taste him.

"And each time you come, you're going to tell me who owns you, body and soul."

Oh shit. She couldn't do that. She wasn't ever going to admit another feeling to him.

She tried to tell him off, but it came out as "wumph heph fwee owr".

"What was that? Was that 'when hell freezes over'?"

She nodded frantically, more turned on that he'd understood. Who was she kidding? A man who knew her in such a way was as priceless to her as Royal.

Ten taps on each cheek. When she felt her spine sagging into the mattress and the sheets growing damp from her juices, her mind blanked and she knew only Ty.

His warm, rough hands on her, the way he brought her to orgasm not once with the vibrator but twice. When he buried his tongue in her pussy, she gave herself totally.

Small squeaks left her, muffled by the gag. But if he knew her well enough, he'd know she was telling him she loved him. Over and over.

When he brought her to the next peak, he said it back, "I love you too, baby girl."

* * * * *

Using controlled movements, Ty shed his clothes. He kept his gaze locked on Bree's sleek curves as he rounded the bed, cock in hand. He stroked it in front of her, watching her eyes darken as the tip beaded with precome.

"You want to suck it, don't you?" He'd already conquered her, but he needed to give her some control. This was their game and they both needed it. Only when they lay sated in each other's arms could they truly have everything they wanted.

She nodded, blushing. He stroked her hair off her face and removed the gag. She wet her lips and he bent to taste their sweet plumpness. He bit back a groan.

Holding his cock at the root, he pressed it against her lips. She mewled and opened. "All the way, baby. You know I'm thick. Yes, that's it. Gawwwd." His balls clenched as he found himself buried in her hot, wet mouth.

She hollowed her cheeks and sucked. His position and her being tied to the bed didn't make it easy for him to get the angle he needed, but that was a good thing. If she sucked him the way he wanted, he'd never last. When he came, it was going to be in her sweet pussy.

His legs started to weaken. She made a noise, and he withdrew, stomach pitching. Breathing heavily, he touched the rope on her wrist. "Do you want to be untied for this?"

"Yes," she rasped.

Good. He wanted to feel her arms around him.

He unbound her arms and legs then rubbed them lightly to get the blood flowing. She pushed upward until her ass waved in the air.

"You're begging for it, aren't you, baby girl? Tell me what you want this time."

"I want...can I have...I've been naughty enough for another spanking."

Ffffuck. His mind whirled. That she gave him all the control made him burn up. "Yesss, you have. Like this?" He spanked her too lightly.

"Ungh."

"This?" He slapped her a little harder, lifting the cheek on his palm and loving how it jiggled as it fell.

She shook her head.

"Maybe harder. How bad have you been?"

"Do I need...to tell you?"

His cock was steely, purple and oozing precome. He lost it. Reddening both cheeks and spanking her pussy several times until she was soaking wet. Then he rolled her onto her back and covered her with his body.

"I thought you wanted to feel how hot my ass was when you took me," she said.

"I changed my mind. I need to see your eyes when I come in you."

Her lips fell open and a gorgeous glow stole over her skin as she watched him slide a condom into place. Then he gathered her to his chest and sank deep.

* * * * *

Bree's walls clenched around Ty's invasion. She dug her nails into his scalp and found his mouth. In a rush of love and need, she kissed him. His tongue skated along hers as he slowly, thoroughly fucked her. But this was so much more than pleasure.

"You said you love me."

"I do." He angled upward, catching the perfect spot. She gasped and clung tighter.

"Say it again."

"No demands out of you, baby girl. Okay, just this once. I love you, Bree Now tell me what you want from me."

"I want you to make me come." She sucked in sharply as he plunged so deep she had no idea where she ended and he began.

"And?" He bit her nipple, and she arched.

"And you to tell me your favorite meal."

"Baked potatoes."

"With bacon and cheese?"

"And chives and sour cream."

She held his gaze, on the verge of dropping into a chasm bigger than anything she'd ever navigated before. She was ready — in all ways.

"I want you to give up your job for me, Ty."

He stilled inside her. Their gazes connected and so many unspoken things were understood all of a sudden. "Already have." He grunted and shoved her up the bed.

She held on to him as he took her hard and fast, sucking her nipples. Pressure mounted and the inner quake took hold. When intense waves crashed over her, he claimed her mouth, and she poured herself into the kiss. Showing him just how good they could be together.

Epilogue

At the sound of hooves, Ty looked up. Bree was sailing across the field on the back of Royal. He shook his head as she did a trick, whirling and seating herself backward.

"At least she isn't standing," Lissy said. She'd saved Bree's horse and for that Ty would always have a soft spot for the woman. He'd help build her twenty porches in thanks.

"As if you can talk, Lissy. Half the time you've got me all tied in knots because you're jumping everything in sight." Paul switched the hammer to the other hand to draw Lissy into a kiss.

Ty wandered away from the wide porch he was helping to build. Bree righted herself in the saddle and slowed Royal. He met her in the yard.

"You know better than to trespass on this land." He grinned at her.

She swiped at him, but he danced out of the way. "I'm delivering a message. Since you left your cell phone at the cabin."

They'd been staying in the trapper's cabin. It was far from comfortable and more like camping out, but they were alone.

"Couldn't find it."

They shared a knowing smile. He hadn't been able to find the phone because he'd thrown his clothes all over the place after coming in from a hard day's work. Between the Roberts ranch and the Boot Knockers Ranch, he was always busy.

"Hugh called. He wants you in his office."

He sighed. Hugh and Riggs had granted him a longer leave of absence but he'd known this day would be coming. He was either in or out.

"Thanks, Bree." He accepted his cell and returned the hammer to the toolbox. He looked to Paul. "I'll be back. Gotta see the boss man."

"Good luck. And if you see Jack in the valley, tell him we need him."

Lissy flushed, and Ty hid his smile.

"Will do."

He walked to his own horse and slipped into the saddle. Bree rode up to him, close enough he could pull her across his lap if he wanted.

"Should I ride with you?"

"Can if you'd like. I need to talk to Hugh alone, though."

"Okay." They trotted down the slope and across the long field to the main buildings. Ty set his jaw. What if he was told to leave the ranch? The Boot Knockers didn't need more ranch hands. And if he wasn't taking on clients, he wasn't doing the ranch any good.

He left Bree outside the barn. Seeing the tension on her beautiful features, he sent her a wink. "Don't pick up any men while you're waiting."

"Come on, Ty. You know you're secretly hoping I bring a man home to you."

His jeans grew a little tighter. "You do know me, baby girl. But I say who and when."

She bit into her lower lip, giving him that look that revealed how much she loved when he took control.

He stamped a kiss to her full lips. "Be good."

"Are you kidding me? Around all these cowboys?" she sassed.

Shaking his head, he walked the short distance to the office. Hugh and Riggs were digging through a box of paperwork, their heads bent close. Maybe at some point he and Bree would add a third to their relationship, but for now he wanted her all to himself.

His cock was still half-hard at the suggestion she'd made about bringing home a cowboy. *Well, maybe not* all *to myself.*

His bosses looked up.

"Bree said you called for me."

"We did."

Ty started to sink into the seat and Hugh said, "No need to sit. We need your body on this side of the desk."

Confusion pulled Ty's brows together. "What?"

"This box is one of the things that will be your duty. I can't make sense of the contents." Riggs's crooked smile was contagious but Ty shook his head, not understanding.

Hugh leveled his gaze on Ty. "We're in need of a ranch manager."

His heart kicked into a faster speed. "I don't understand. You're the manager."

"I manage the guys. Riggs sees to the grounds. We have other personnel for taking care of the clients and applications and matching women to Boot Knockers. But we need someone else to control the land and how it's used. The money end of the whole operation—cattle, land and Boot Knockers. It's a big job but you *were* valedictorian."

Ty stared, unable to process what was happening. He'd come in here expecting to lose his place, the only place he'd ever really belonged, besides with Bree.

"You know I come as a package deal," he said.

"Yeah, that's why we're giving you a bungalow." Riggs twitched his head toward the window and the line of red roofs.

Ty's eyes bulged.

"Bungalow 20."

"The new one?"

"Until you and Bree decide where you want to build."

"If you want to build."

Ty scuffed his jaw. "I think we will want that. And soon." He couldn't stop his smile. "I asked her to marry me."

Hugh reached across the desk. Ty took his hand and shook it. Then he allowed Hugh to pull him across — to the other side of the business. "Welcome aboard, Ty."

Riggs dangled a key in his face. "Bungalow 20 awaits. Go get your gal and tell her the good news."

As Ty accepted the small brass key, total happiness settled over him. Now all he needed was for his hellion fiancée to get a little mouthy.

THE END

Read on for a peek at ROPE BURN, Book 5 of The Boot Knockers Ranch series

"Ms. Tracy? Tabbart?"

The cautious voice made Tabbart pivot in her makeup chair. Her gaze fell on a young woman who, judging by the notepad and pen in her hand, could only be a fan.

Tabbart waved away the artist applying mascara to her already long lashes and gestured the woman to come into the room. "Hi, what's your name?"

"S-Sarah. I'm such a fan! Oh my God, you're even more beautiful in person!"

Tabbart had heard it all before—from producers, fellow chefs in the television industry and even magazine photographers. But the way people viewed her always came as a shock. Sure, she was a household name. She had a collection of food on the store shelves and cooking utensils on QVC. But deep down, she was just plain old Tabbart.

"Would you like me to sign that, Sarah?"

The young woman's eyes fired with excitement and she bounced on the toes of her Converse sneakers. "Yes! I'd love that. You're my idol. I have my own cooking show on YouTube and I try to channel the energy you put into your shows. I hope to someday cook delicious food like you do."

Tabbart almost laughed. For all Sarah knew, everything Tabbart cooked in front of the live audience and cameras tasted like plastic. Tabbart was known as a top chef, but very few people had actually sampled food created by her hands.

"Are you here in the audience today?" she asked as she scrawled her name across the sheet of paper—*To Sarah. Always cook with passion. —Tabbart Tracy.*

"Yes!"

Tabbart looked around at her assistant, who was flipping through clothes on a long rack, selecting Tabbart's wardrobe for today's show. "Mindy, would you mind showing Sarah to the VIP room and letting her sample the buffet?"

For some reason it was very important that Sarah walked out of the studio today believing in Tabbart's abilities offscreen as well as on. If the young woman truly did desire a career in cooking, she needed to realize what went on behind the camera was more important than in front of it.

Too bad not many cared.

Sarah squealed. "Oh, it's your food, isn't it? I'd be so honored to sample your cooking, Ms. Tracy!"

Tabbart smiled at her enthusiasm. "I hope you enjoy it." The makeup artist came at her from the side with the mascara wand again.

"Thank you so much, Ms. Tracy," Sarah gushed as Mindy led her from the room.

"Thank you for believing in me," Tabbart murmured as the door closed.

For the four years she'd been a TV food star, she'd met dozens of girls like Sarah. She always took time for them, and not only because the paparazzi would love to capture her being a total bitch. No, Tabbart had once been one of those girls—enthusiastic, hungry for a show on national TV and her name in every home in America.

"Mindy's selected the blue sweater for you today," the artist said with one last pat of powder to her nose and cheeks, ensuring the stage lights didn't make her appear too shiny on camera.

Tabbart sighed. She was sick and tired of blue. The network put her in blue three times a week. The packaging of her cookware was even blue. It shouldn't matter, except she had little say.

Or maybe she did. Somewhere along the way she'd quit caring.

As the artist assisted Tabbart out of her robe and into the blue sweater with jeweled buttons, she said, "This royal blue makes your skin glow. If you ever decide to get married, forget white. Blue is your color."

Fat chance I'll ever get married. She was thirty-four years old and hadn't dated seriously in two years. When fame had first struck, she'd been on dates with a film actor with a career much, much bigger than his personality—and cock. A hockey star and even another TV chef. Then she'd turned to dating a studio executive. That had lasted the longest and seemed the most promising—it had taken him exactly a month before he expected her to serve him homemade pies in the nude.

As she turned to the mirror surrounded by fat bulbs, she gazed at her reflection. Dark, glossy hair waving over her shoulders and brown eyes highlighted by enormous lashes. In person they looked over the top, but on camera, they'd be perfect. She sighed. After the show, another magazine would probably ask her for a guest feature in which she provided makeup tips.

Just once she'd like to tell the magazine editor that she didn't know jack shit about applying more than a smear of lipstick. When she was off camera, she didn't wear any.

Mindy returned as Tabbart was stepping into a flared skirt with a graphic white-and-black pattern. "You look perfect. Now for the heels."

Tabbart preferred flat shoes for cooking, but being on the shorter side of five feet, she required high heels for the set. She stepped into the designer leather that molded to her feet perfectly.

For a moment she twisted her foot side to side, admiring the shoes. "I love these." Shoes were one of the few things she liked about getting primped for a taping.

"I knew you would." Mindy smiled and knelt to fiddle with the pleats in Tabbart's skirt.

Two raps on the door. "Five minutes, Tabbart."

Tabbart's brain blanked suddenly. What was she even cooking today? She cast her mind about the week's schedule. She had created the menu and damn if she could remember. After forty weeks of meal plans for the past four years, the dishes all ran together.

"Is today the guest chef from the Hilton Head Hotel?"

Mindy exchanged a look with the makeup artist. "No. It's seafood day."

"Oh yes." Baked stuffed Maine lobster tails, an appetizer of mussels in garlic butter and a summer pilaf. Dessert was... She racked her brain. What was wrong with her?

Burnout. She was one of the few people in this industry who worked so hard. While many had twenty-four weeks of shows, she had forty. Her downtime consisted of QVC appearances and traveling to get inspiration for new dishes. She hadn't had a proper vacation since...

Since a lonely trip to the Maldives. She'd hoped to lie on the beach and rest, maybe dance the night away with a tall, dark and hung vacationer, but she'd spent most of her time writing new recipes in her journal.

Citron splash martini with a twist. That was her dessert—a cocktail.

She'd need it after this taping, if she continued to be so unfocused.

The minute she stepped out of her dressing room, her brain returned. She followed the stage manager through the maze of hallways leading to the set. The lights raised the temps about thirty degrees. Why had they put her in a sweater? Her wardrobe didn't even match her food today. A seafood dish in a sweater and flared skirt? She glanced down at herself. Well, she did look as if she'd walked out of the Hamptons.

"Five, four, three…"

Her mind zeroed in on the task before her. Onstage she was in her element. Comfortable, engaging the live audience as well as the television one. She pasted a smile in place and stepped out.

* * * * *

Stowe watched the woman cross the stage to the set kitchen. Her warm dark-brown hair gleamed under the bright lights. She moved with a fluid grace and knew how to work a pair of heels. He dropped his gaze to her lean calves. She was a runner.

His mind automatically reached for her file. In his line of work, every woman who set foot onstage had a file — photo, application, history. And several paragraphs on her needs.

But not this one. He wasn't on the Boot Knockers Ranch today.

As he watched the TV chef take her place behind a long marble countertop, he studied her face. Not a hint of fear or nervousness shone there. Yeah, he was far from home. Each lady visiting the ranch got onstage to be chosen by a cowboy who would entertain her for a week. Very few weren't nervous.

His sister Amelia stood at his side, arms folded, smiling at a joke the TV food star had made after introducing her menu. When Amelia had asked him to join her at her workplace for a few hours, he'd been happy to see what his li'l sis did with her talents on a daily basis.

It didn't shock him that she was behind the scenes in this type of business. In contrast, he was front stage, center, in his line of work. Yeah, he was far from his element today.

No cowboys were within a country mile of this Hollywood set. He felt out of place in his black Aussie cowboy hat with the scalloped band. Not to mention his black boots. Out of respect for Amelia, he'd worn tailored black dress pants and a white button-down shirt. He didn't want to embarrass her by looking like a bumpkin relation.

The woman onstage—what was her name? Tabbart Tracy—smiled and nodded. Her hands moved as if they belonged to another person. She really had control of herself in front of the audience and cameras and knew how to entertain while cooking. She pulled a big knife from a wooden block and began to chop shallots.

He rocked back on his heels and studied her. It wasn't his job to analyze her, but it was hard to remove himself from his own work. He'd gotten so good at it, he could usually glance at a woman and see what she needed, what she was missing in her life.

As a sex therapist, he treated a lot of control freaks—especially in his area of specialty. They didn't call him the Dom from Down Under for nothing. He spent a lot of time on a stage under hot lights too, teaching women control and submission. And often women in positions of tight control needed to let loose — to give some up.

Amelia whispered something into the headset she wore, then shot Stowe a look. *I'll be right back,* she mouthed. She slinked into the shadows to take care of a job duty, leaving Stowe to watch.

Tabbart held up the knife and pointed to the flat of the blade before crushing it against something on the cutting board. The scent of garlic reached him, making his stomach rumble.

That was something he missed about the BK Ranch — home-cooking. Amelia was no master of the hot plate in her little one-room apartment. Stowe had been eating soup and toast since his arrival. He could afford to treat them both to several meals a day, but his sister wouldn't let him spend his hard-earned money. She was frugal like their mother.

A trace of homesickness passed over him. Actually, since hearing Amelia's Australian accent, he'd been overwhelmed with the feeling. Texas had been his home for several years but he missed his family. Having a link to Amelia in the same country felt good, and he wished he could visit her more often. Except LA wasn't exactly his thing.

Tabbart swirled a spoon in a bowl and then brought it to her lips. Lush lips, full and kissable, stained red. He shifted from boot to boot, his trousers suddenly tighter. He loved having a woman's red lipstick smeared all over him—mouth, neck, chest and a ring around his cock.

Amelia returned and he tamped down his thoughts. His sister knew what he did for a living, but he tried not to be a horndog while visiting her. He had crazy-hot sex too many weeks a year to count. He could take a few days off.

Then Tabbart ran her pink tongue over her lower lip. On the huge monitor in front of him, the action was amplified. In a blink, he was rock hard.

Damn.

She was pretty but he had no intention of acting on it. He'd just have to take care of himself once he was alone in the shower tonight.

As Tabbart moved through preparations of the appetizer to the main dish, he leaned close to Amelia.

"Isn't she great?" Amelia whispered.

He nodded. "Is she single?"

She punched him in the arm and one of the cameramen shot them a grin. "You'd better be kidding."

"I am." Sort of. Tabbart's smile beckoned on the monitor. Too easily he saw her strapped to the St. Andrew's Cross, giving him that coaxing smile. Charming him even as he punished her for disobedience.

He shook himself.

Time to focus on anything but the beautiful star. He wasn't interested in a one-night stand, or anything else for that matter. He was here to find his roots with his sister again.

"I hope you have a nice dress," he said to Amelia.

Her eyes widened and she gave him her full attention. "Why?"

"I have tickets to *Calamity Jane*."

"The musical?" She sounded like a little girl on Christmas morning.

He nodded.

"Wow, I haven't been to any performance since coming out here. I thought I'd have all the time and money to experience the city's cultures, and here I am years later, living on ramen noodles."

"We have dinner reservations too."

Her eyes sparkled. "You're full of surprises. Except one."

"What's that?"

"*Calamity Jane*? You just can't get enough of being a cowboy, can you?"

"Never." Pride filled him. Back in Australia he'd rodeo'd. Once he'd hit American soil, he'd thought work would be easy to come by. Ranching work meant busting his ass for long hours and low pay. Stowe knew he was cut out for something better. That's when Hugh had found him and offered him a job at the Boot Knockers Ranch.

He loved wielding a whip for a living, using his knowledge of the BDSM life every day. He had great friends and a true love of Texas. But he'd been ready for a break. After one female client a few months ago, he'd lost a little passion.

Watching Tabbart carefully concoct a buttery sauce to drizzle over the stuffed lobster, he drifted in memories of that client. She'd been a sub abandoned by her Dom. He'd welcomed the challenge of fulfilling her need to please and serve. Trouble was, it had knocked him off balance.

Amelia slipped away on another errand and he turned his attention to Tabbart. Her beauty was arresting. If he saw her in the supermarket in sweats, she'd still be beautiful. Her coiffed hair was on one monitor and a perfect manicure on another as she worked. Both could go and she'd still be lovely.

That was it—she had a femininity he rarely saw. Some women possessed it without effort. Grace Kelly was a good example, and Tabbart had an old-Hollywood glamour.

With a smile and flourish, she placed her lobster tail in a wall oven. A crew member called a cut. Tabbart took a sip from a bottled water hidden somewhere out of sight. As she wrapped her lips around the bottle, his erection returned full force.

God, he was conditioned to need sex and kink all the time. He'd probably be turned on by the grizzled old stagecoach driver in the musical tonight.

Tabbart allowed an assistant to powder her face and spoke animatedly with a producer on set. Then she came out from behind the counter and spoke to the audience. Talking to a few women in the front row, signing autographs. She seemed genuinely happy to meet her fans.

"Seven minutes till we roll," someone announced. Tabbart looked up and nodded. Her glance moved over Stowe standing in the shadows.

He stared at her for a long heartbeat, aware of how delicate her features were. Arching brows, small nose that hadn't been touched by a surgeon's knife. And those plump lips that had his engine revving.

She drew a breath big enough that her breasts swelled. He flicked his gaze downward, licking over them to her tiny waist. Her hips were obscured by the floaty skirt, but he'd bet his favorite cat-o'-nine-tails whip that her hips were fuller. Her bottom perfect for grabbing and tugging her into his cock.

"Five minutes."

Good Christ. Had they really been staring at each other for two minutes? He gave her a nod and fingered the brim of his hat. A smile teased the corner of her lips, but she didn't shine that smile on him.

Someone else claimed her attention and she swung away. In seconds she was positioned behind the counter again, barricaded from him.

For the rest of the taping, he tried to get his hormones under control. Damn, he was like a randy goat, willing to fuck anything within grasp.

That wasn't exactly true. He looked at the women in the front of the audience. Some more attractive than others. Each and every one of them he could make drop to their knees and pant with need after a few orders. But he didn't have any desire to try.

Actually, since the sub he'd helped on the ranch, he hadn't felt empty.

Tabbart prepared rice pilaf and then nibbled a bite of mussels in garlic butter, her square white teeth working the edge of the food until his balls clenched. He longed to shove his hands through her thick, shining hair and muss it. To see her undone would be the perfect challenge right now.

As the woman produced a martini glass and a bottle of vodka, he felt a bead of sweat trickle into his shirt collar. She wielded the bottle like a pro, adding a dash of this and that.

Hell, he didn't even know what. All he knew was when she brought the glass to her lips and closed her eyes at the first sip, he needed to get out of there before he embarrassed himself.

And Amelia.

She put her hand on his arm, jerking his attention from the up-close-and-tormenting view of Tabbart's lips on the monitor.

"I have some things to do after the taping. There might be a few retakes, but I don't think so. Tabbart did great."

"She did."

"Hang out here and we'll see if I can introduce you to her."

"Yeah, I'd like that."

Amelia bobbed out of sight. The filming wrapped up. Tabbart hung out to sign a few autographs in the audience. Then trays of the mussels she'd cooked today revolved through the fans. When Stowe plucked a toothpick-speared appetizer off the tray, he glanced up to find the woman holding the tray staring.

"Thank you," he rumbled before popping the food in his mouth. Flavors burst on his tongue. God, after several days of canned soup, it tasted like heaven.

"You're from Australia," the woman commented.

He chewed and swallowed. "Yep."

"Say something in Australian."

He bit off a laugh. How many times had he encountered people who believed he spoke a different language? He conjured his best accent and said, "I believe after several of these, I'd be as full as a centipede's sock drawer."

The woman batted her lashes and he chuckled. "I just love a man with an accent." She moved on, offering someone else a mussel.

He glanced up in time to see Tabbart's back as she was ushered off the set. He gnawed on the toothpick in the corner of his mouth and waited for his sister to return. Several minutes later she appeared beside him, eyes sparkling.

"I've arranged a meeting with Tabbart. Now don't be nervous. She's as sweet as pie."

Those two words couldn't be uttered together without him thinking of dirty things. He grinned around the toothpick and followed Amelia backstage through a series of hallways.

As they passed a couple of women wearing headsets and holding clipboards, the women stopped talking and snapped their heads around. Amelia groaned and murmured, "I forgot how women act like drooling idiots around you."

"I can't help it."

"Yeah, but you don't exactly downplay your looks, brother." She reached for a doorknob and twisted it.

Stowe followed her inside a spacious room painted red. Groups of people clustered, some holding plates of food from the buffet along one wall.

"You must be Amelia's brother from Down Under." A young blonde laughed at her own rhyming joke. She stuck her hand right into his, catching his eyes and giving her best impression of a toothpaste ad model.

He shook her hand and spoke with her while Amelia rolled her eyes. He gave the blonde all the attention she craved before two other women angled for him. Pretty soon he was surrounded by ladies.

Amelia reached between them and gripped Stowe's arm. She tugged. "Excuse us, but I'd like my brother to meet someone."

He broke free of the knot of teased hair and lipstick. Stowe's gaze locked on the curvy backside of the TV chef. She stood at the buffet, dumping vodka into martini glasses.

"Tabbart, I'd like you to meet my brother."

The woman pivoted. Her gaze locked on Stowe and she dribbled some vodka onto the white tablecloth lining the buffet. "Oh." She settled the bottle on the surface and made a show of drying her hands on a cloth. Avoiding his gaze.

He looked at her closer. Maybe she wasn't as in control as he'd first believed. Her hands shook and a pretty pink blush coated her cheeks.

He knew how to soothe a jittery woman, especially one he pictured tied spread-eagle on his bed.

He swooped in and removed the cloth from her. After setting it aside, he gathered both of her hands between his and gazed into her eyes.

Em Petrova

Em Petrova was raised by hippies in the wilds of Pennsylvania but told her parents at the age of four she wanted to be a gypsy when she grew up. She has a soft spot for babies, puppies and 90s Grunge music and believes in Bigfoot and aliens. She started writing at the age of twelve and prides herself on making her characters larger than life and her sex scenes hotter than hot.

She burst into the world of publishing in 2010 after having five beautiful bambinos and figuring they were old enough to get their own snacks while she pounds away at the keys. In her not-so-spare time, she is fur-mommy to a Labradoodle named Daisy Hasselhoff and works as editor with USA Today and New York Times bestselling authors.

Find Em Petrova at http://empetrova.com

The Boot Knocker Ranch Series
PUSHIN' BUTTONS
BODY LANGUAGE
REINING MEN
ROPIN' HEARTS
ROPE BURN
COWBOY NOT INCLUDED

Country Fever Series
HARD RIDIN'
LIP LOCK
UNBROKEN
SOMETHIN' DIRTY

Rope 'n Ride Series
BUCK
RYDER
RIDGE
WEST
LANE
WYNONNA

Rope 'n Ride On Series
JINGLE BOOTS

DOUBLE DIPPIN'
LICKS AND PROMISES
A COWBOY FOR CHRISTMAS
LIPSTICK 'N LEAD

The Dalton Boys
COWBOY CRAZY Hank's story
COWBOY BARGAIN Cash's story
COWBOY CRUSHIN' Witt's story
COWBOY SECRET Beck's story
COWBOY RUSH Kade's Story

Single Titles and Boxes
STRANDED AND STRADDLED
LASSO MY HEART
SINFUL HEARTS
BLOWN DOWN
FALLEN
FEVERED HEARTS
DIRTY HAIR PULLER

Firehouse 5 Series
ONE FIERY NIGHT
CONTROLLED BURN
SMOLDERING HEARTS

The Quick and the Hot Series
DALLAS NIGHTS
SLICK RIDER
SPURRED ON

Also, look for traditionally published works on her website.

Made in United States
Orlando, FL
08 August 2023

35891239R00189